IN SEARCH OF LEO

ANITHA KRISHNAN

DREAM PEDLAR PUBLICATIONS

Ebook ISBN: 978-1-7752278-0-9

Paperback ISBN: 978-1-7388158-2-1

Edited by Sarah Chorn

Cover Design by Pen Astridge

❀ Created with Vellum

For all who grieve the loss of someone or something they dearly loved.

And for all who grieve without quite knowing why.

~

For Abhinav and Dhruv,
who show me every day how to live and how to love.

ABOUT THIS BOOK

In Search of Leo

When you lose someone you love, how far would you go in search of them?

And what if the only way you can find them is by first losing yourself along the way?

Devastated by grief at the loss of her beloved dog, Leo, Heidi ventures into the woods behind her home, hoping to find him there.

She meets strange and eccentric characters along the way, but no one seems inclined to give her a straight answer about Leo's whereabouts.

Frustrated and confused, Heidi begins to wonder if there is more to these characters than meets the eye. The Oldest Witch who lives in a snow bubble of denial. The Omniscient

Man who trivializes Heidi's pain. The lonely woman, Gaia, who is consumed by anger. And many others.

As Heidi struggles to make sense of their cryptic responses, she must also navigate her own emotions and face up to the distinct possibility she has been refusing to consider all along. Perhaps Leo is truly gone forever and she may never find him.

Drifting from one dreamlike encounter to another, Heidi discovers that the journey through grief, from loss towards acceptance, is a meandering. It unfolds of its own accord, often seemingly without purpose or reason. But can she survive it without first getting hopelessly lost?

FOREWORD

This is not a story. This is an acid trip.

The kind you'd go on when you're trying to avoid feeling your feelings.

Which is also precisely the kind of trip you'd go on when you're feeling your feelings instead.

In both cases, you're in the throes of an inexplicable delirium.

Words and imagery tumble and collide into each other. Nothing makes sense. Yet, it all makes perfect sense. Until you try to explain it to someone else, that is. And then it all goes back to seeming nonsensical somehow.

Grief is one such phenomenon. It cannot be comprehended or explained in words and images. It cannot be analyzed or reasoned with. It cannot be deconstructed into constituent elements or broken down into a formula or depicted as an equation. It can only be experienced.

Yet, in the pages that follow, I have attempted to depict some of the various well-known stages of grief against the backdrop of fantasy.

In an act of audacity, I have personified these feelings using various fictional characters and their eccentricities.

Denial is the Oldest Witch who lives in her snow bubble.

Spiritual bypassing is the Omniscient Man who is moved by the sorrows of the collective world but refuses to acknowledge the overwhelming grief of an individual.

Anger is the woman, Gaia, who burns down her home and farmland following her loss and continues to live in her singed world, stubbornly refusing to forgive.

I wrote this tale to cope with my own grief after going through a very difficult period of estrangement and unexpected loss.

Grief hurts. A hell of a lot.

It becomes a meandering. A floundering. A search for meaning. A search for some noble purpose to explain all the pain. A purpose that may or may not exist, although the pain does.

Acceptance comes as a salve in its own sweet time. It can be neither prescribed nor forced. It will simply not be rushed.

Yet, it doesn't depict an ending of grief either. But it profoundly changes our relationship with grief, rendering it an acceptable and bearable lifelong companion now.

But all books come to an end. And this one does too, but on a hopeful note.

My hope is for you to find within these pages permission to lose yourself in beautiful words and wild symbolisms, even though they are at best an approximation of the sorrow that ravages you.

In the end, I hope you find that grief has loosened its unrelenting grip on your soul somewhat and that you can go forth in life without having to clutch at your broken heart every time it beats.

~ Anitha Krishnan
Burlington, Ontario
18 January 2023

A STRANGE ENCOUNTER

PROLOGUE

Heidi was returning from a burial on the hilltop, contemplating the relative merits and demerits of death, when the man emerged from behind a cluster of trees.

It took her a few moments to register his presence, so lost was she in her thoughts on dying and the dead.

Death by age.

Endings by desire.

Eternal rest by volition, one's own or another's.

Lives cut short by accident or by illness. How much longer would they have lasted anyway?

Slow deaths. Swift departures.

Peaceful demises. Violent ends.

It was almost as if death did not want to be outdone by life in its flair for vagary.

Well, it was too late to entertain these thoughts now, for she had made up her mind and the deed had been done.

And so, the sudden appearance of the stranger did not startle her. There was nothing he could possibly take from her now. She had touched the face of death and had nothing more to lose.

He was dressed simply. Blue jeans and a white T-shirt with a print on the front that was partly obscured by a black jacket. Red and white sneakers. He looked so ordinary.

He moved his lips but the words that fell upon her ears were garbled, as if they had travelled underwater.

They made even less sense when she thought about them later and tried to comprehend their meaning.

The Dream Pedlar.

The Hidden Moon.

The man stepped forward and pressed something cold and hard into her palm.

Heidi looked down to find a heart-shaped bottle of frosted glass. In it swished a liquid of Prussian blue, like small waves rippling the surface of a palm-sized ocean, occasionally revealing an arc of silver.

The man said something about an elixir, a cure for pain and loss, a nostrum for grief and sorrow.

Heidi caught a few more words drifting in the breeze. *Life. Worth fighting for.*

The bottle of nectar in her hand felt heavy as if laden with some unspoken promise. She looked at the man, and wondered. A cure for loss? She was desperate for hope but reluctant to believe in a miracle that was yet to come true.

But the man nodded, in understanding and in endorsement. His unexpected gesture of confirmation dispelled all thoughts of death from Heidi's mind and planted a tiny sprig of faith in there.

She threw back her head and emptied the tiny bottle in one gulp. The liquid was cool when it glided down her throat, but almost instantly a pleasant sensation of warmth coursed through her veins and settled under her skin.

This was a serendipitous gift from the Universe, Heidi thought, invigorating like the first drop of rain landing splat on her outstretched arm, and then protective like a fireside keeping her warm in a storm. Her heart broke into a birdsong.

Perhaps it wasn't too late after all. Perhaps she could still save Leo. The thought made her so giddy with hope she ran back home faster than the wind.

CHAPTER I
THE WOODS, MOONLIGHT, AND MR. FOX

Leo's leash lay on the porch. A squiggly sash of brown on white floorboards. Abandoned. It looked like a dead snake.

It was still hooked to the collar at one end. Missing its wearer, the contraption looked like a lasso, Heidi noticed.

It was limp and useless now, with no one to rein in. As if the old boy had somehow shrunk and wriggled out of the restraint and had bounded away towards mischief.

A tightness tugged at Heidi's gut and moved up to squeeze her chest. Terror and guilt collided in the very centre of her being. Every breath of air whooshed out of her. Her throat constricted and her jaws clamped shut.

She would have stood at her porch for a very long time, not knowing what to do next. But the realization that Leo was missing sent her zigzagging from her front yard to the village centre, from the baker's to the grocer's, from her neighbour's to her friends' in the next village.

A couple of hours of futile pursuit later, she conceded Leo

must have run off to the one place he knew better than to have ventured into alone. The woods.

Back home, Heidi packed a torch, a loaf of bread left over from yesterday's supper, two bars of Mars chocolate, a flask of spiced tea, and a bottle of water in a knapsack. She heaved it on to her shoulder and let herself out through the back door.

The woods, once upon a time a coppice, began where the lawn in her backyard now refused to be mowed. No fence was required to slice the land into proprietorial zones. None could keep the forest away.

Heidi strode through the overgrown grass and disappeared into the woods just as the periwinkle sky was beginning to shed its flimsy colours and give way to the blackness of the night.

It was summer in the village but an in-between season in the woods. Not quite fall. Not quite spring. Summer and winter were playing hide and seek, both uncertain whose turn it was to hide and whose to seek.

"Leo, Leo," Heidi called out and flicked on her torch.

Light gushed onto a small patch ahead of her but the surrounding area grew darker, as if all the light of the forest was converging in that compact pool. She pointed the beam to the left and right, near and far. Forest-things scuttled out of view.

The last thing she wanted to do was scare Leo away with a strange tube of light that was too bright, too unfamiliar for him to want to reveal himself. She threw the torch back into her knapsack.

She might as well get used to seeing by the feeble light of the night. She hadn't brought any spare batteries after all.

"Leo, Leo," Heidi hollered as she made her way. Her voice

ricocheted off tree trunks. Echoes reverberated around her briefly, then lost themselves to the muddy earth and the opaque air of the night.

"Leo, Leo," she called out again. Each cry momentarily interrupted the sylvan nocturne.

Cicadas ceased to shriek. Frogs paused mid-croak. The wind dropped. Restless, rustling leaves cut short their gossip. Owls swivelled their heads noiselessly. Wolf-howls hung from the still breeze in anticipation. Twigs underfoot failed to snap.

The earth adjourned its motion for half a moment like a ballerina halted in mid-pirouette. The universe allowed an interlude for Leo, but he did not respond.

Time moved by a deft hand, and all the nocturnal sounds rose and rushed and surged and roared again all at once, resurrected just as swiftly and abruptly as they had ceased.

Deeper and deeper into the woods Heidi ventured, sparing little thought to how far she had come or how much further she would have to go, or how she would find her way back home. But the brute force of terror, on the strength of which she had begun her journey, was rapidly crumbling.

Something combative had held her together and kept her on her feet thus far. Something resolute and steady had propelled her through the woods until now, but it was quickly unravelling.

The blood that had drummed in her ears and throbbed in her head back at the porch now pooled onerously around her ankles, like dead weight.

Her feet and boots felt like misshapen boulders, plotting to trip her up and slow her down. Her back and shoulders stooped under the weight of her knapsack, like reeds that bowed to the wind.

Her throat was flayed by her insistent cries to Leo, and wouldn't be soothed by the mouthfuls of water she gulped from her bottle until it was nearly empty. Her voice had whittled down to a hoarse unfamiliar whisper she worried Leo wouldn't recognize.

She felt unmoored. Like a fallen leaf of autumn being whisked away by a frosty wind.

Heidi ran into a tree and slumped against its trunk. She was spent. Shattered. She let herself slip into a downward spiral of exhaustion, weighed down by tired bones and jagged breath and a splintered spirit.

She kicked off her boots, dropped her knapsack, and curled up in a foetal position. Thighs pressed to her chest, she buried her face between her knees. And for the first time since her mother had died, Heidi began to cry.

Her tears resolutely found a way to bleed through eyes shut tight. Sorrow trickled from a dark, lonely place lodged deep within her and rattled her entire being.

"Stupid, stupid boy," Heidi said softly into her knees. Perhaps he was home right now, she thought hopefully. Maybe he was back on the porch, wondering where *she* was.

There were other possibilities too, she knew, grim prospects she couldn't bear to think about even though they whispered and thrummed in her subconscious like a plainsong throbbing inside the walls of a cathedral.

She wrapped her arms around her knees and pulled herself into a tight ball, as if to keep all the dark thoughts from coming in, as if to keep herself from falling to bits.

Which is why she didn't hear the fox approach. Nor did she see him at first.

When she finally felt she could loosen up a little without

losing her composure, she looked up and saw that the forest had changed.

Where once everything had been painted in different shades of sable, the moon now peeked from behind clouds and leaves, and cast pools of silvery light that swayed on the forest floor in step with the jiggling treetops.

"Beautiful, isn't it?" The words sprang out of the ether beside her.

Heidi whipped her head around. The silhouette of a canid slowly came into view. Shapeshifting spots of moonlight danced on his coat.

Heidi's breath caught in her throat. "Leo," she cried hopefully and jumped up to pull him close and never let go.

But her joy lasted only for as long as that infinite moment. *NotLeoNotLeoNotLeoNotLeo*, a voice rang out in her head.

She stopped herself, arm still outstretched, her mind furiously debating with itself whether or not to reach out towards something, someone that was fast slipping away.

The silhouette made no movement. Its snout stuck out like Pinocchio's nose, Heidi now saw. It was not the boxy maw of her retriever.

Its tail was long and thick, white-tipped, like a paintbrush dipped in moonlight. Nothing like Leo's idiosyncratic comma, a time-halting appendage.

Heidi took a sharp breath. This was no dog that sat beside her. This was a fox.

On any other occasion, Heidi's heart would have been thumping hard and yearning to break free from the restraints of her ribs and scuttle back to the safety of her home in the village. But tonight, she couldn't let fear of the strange and the unfamiliar derail her from her quest.

She merely pulled back her hand and whispered an apology. "Sorry. Sorry. I didn't mean to lunge at you like that. I thought you were Le... I thought you were someone else," she spluttered, disappointed.

The fox sighed. His warm breath tumbled into the cold night. Plumes of pearly silver mist drifted towards the treetops but vanished en route.

"I never thought I'd live to witness something like this," he said, cryptically.

"Witness what?"

"A human," he answered. "In this neck of the woods. So many dangers lurk here even the breeze refuses to pass by."

Heidi looked around her. She felt no fear for herself. "Even a leaf would appear fearsome in the dark." She shrugged.

The fox shook his head. "A human," he said again as if the repetition would settle his incredulity somewhat. "Such a young one that too. Also, polite. And intelligent." Heidi could hear him smile. He turned his head towards her and looked right into her eyes, and gazed into her soul. "Yet you choose to ignore your fear. You either possess extraordinary courage or are an utter imbecile."

Heidi turned the fox's words over in her mind and wondered whether she was being commended or condemned. "I cannot say I agree with you, Mr. erm... Fox. I do not hold extraordinary courage. It is true that I am not afraid of the woods tonight. But that is because I am in the grip of a greater fear. The terror of losing a loved one. And if it is daft of me to go looking for him in forbidden places, well ... there is nothing I wouldn't do for the one I love. If that makes me an utter imbecile, so be it."

The fox nodded, then uttered a single word, with deference. "Leo."

Hope surged within Heidi once more. "Have you seen him, Mr. Fox?" she inquired eagerly. "His fur is the colour of a summer sunset. And his eyes, amber and honey with flecks of liquid gold, are so kind you'd beg to melt in his gaze," she pleaded.

"I haven't had the good fortune of meeting Leo." The fox sounded disappointed to admit. "But I know of your quest. All the creatures of the woods do. The trees, they spread the word," he explained.

Something clicked in Heidi's mind. "Then surely you would know if Leo did wander into the woods. I worry I may not be looking for him in the right places."

The fox looked at her with concern. "The right place is the one where you will stop looking for him. Until you get there, every place will feel wrong. Very wrong."

An uneasy realization dawned on Heidi. Her world had become a strange, unfamiliar place, she began to see.

In her old world, time and space had been neatly defined by precise boundaries.

Her little cottage with its walls and doors and windows and the front porch and backyard, the neighbour's, the village square, the neighbouring village, that was pretty much all she had known her entire life. Every other place was either too far away or swallowed up by the woods, and therefore, no concern of hers.

Now she was journeying through an endless expanse of earth and night sky. She was an ant meandering the Himalayas in the dark.

How long had she been walking? There was no sure way to tell out here in the woods.

Perhaps the fox carried a watch on him and could tell her the time. But could he also tell her how much longer it would take her to find Leo?

A definite length of time, chopped up into hours and minutes and seconds. Unambiguous units of measurement that, for all their mathematical precision, were utterly incapable of illustrating how the moments dragged on when her heart ached, and how they sped up when she was euphoric.

And right now, Leo could be standing at any of the inestimable crossroads of time and space. How could she sift through these unlimited possibilities within the narrow confines of her knowledge, her understanding of a world without him by her side?

And in this not knowing, in this state of aloneness and uncertainty, Heidi saw how fathomless time and space truly were. They refused to be hemmed in. They were impossible to define. Unfurling expansively, running amok, stretching out beyond the horizon, tearing through the skies. Heidi felt small and lost.

"I don't know what to do now, where to look for him," she said softly.

"The Oldest Witch might be able to assist you in your quest," the fox suggested. "She lives in a hidden glade deep within the woods. The pine trees will show you the way."

He then rose, and Heidi thanked him and offered him the loaf of bread from her bag, which he delightedly accepted. He stepped closer to Heidi and rested a paw on her knee. His sock and paw gleamed silver under the moon.

"You have come this far, and that in itself is no mean feat," he gently reminded her. "Countless paths can lead you to the right place. No matter which you choose, each route will first run into a few dead ends, loop back into itself a few times, and lead you to treacherous corners. But keep going, for you have only just begun."

He pressed a wet nose on her shoulder and bounded off. His dark shape disappeared swiftly into the blackness of the forest, like a drop of water dissolving in the ocean.

CHAPTER 2
SNOW, STARS, AND THE OLDEST WITCH

A white picket fence circled the sunlight-speckled glade.

As Heidi approached it, a discarnate voice trilled exuberantly, "Sixteen hours, twenty-six minutes, and four-fifths of a jiffy. That is how long it has taken you from the time you first learnt about me to arrive at my doorstep."

A gate in the fence swung open of its own accord. Heidi entered. The ground that she stepped on trembled ever so slightly, a placid ripple from the core swelling outwards.

All around her rose a giant iridescent bubble, wobbling and billowing until it had cocooned the entire glade. The white pickets crumbled into tiny sand-like grains that blew away like dandelion florets. And it began to snow.

Dainty, white flakes swirled and twirled in an effortless descent. Weightless and benign at first, the snow piled on fast and thick. It covered Heidi's shoes, and settled in the crooks of the naked branches of trees that had sprung up from the ground when she hadn't been looking.

The air turned blue. Heidi was inside a snow globe.

"And that, my dearest, is the fastest I've seen in the past several lustra," the Oldest Witch emerged from behind the trees and smiled at Heidi.

'Oldest', or even 'old', was not the term Heidi would have used to describe the witch. Her skin was fair, poreless like a newborn's. Her cheeks flushed with the colours of eventide. Silvery white tresses swirled down her back. Her eyes sparkled like constellations in a clear, night sky.

Snowdrops sprung up where her feet kissed the ground. She appeared less like a crone and more like a pretty princess trapped by the witch atop a tower. Or inside a snow globe, Heidi thought uneasily.

As the witch drew nearer, Heidi noticed a familiar form of white fur, almost invisible against the snow, striding beside her. A dash of pink in his ears. A dazzle of blue in his eyes. The most handsome Siberian Husky she had ever laid eyes on. Almost Leo. Heidi forgot to breathe for several moments.

"Fuhen has that effect on people," the Oldest Witch said warmly.

"Fuhen," Heidi exhaled. "He is so much like Leo."

The Oldest Witch put her hand on Heidi's shoulder. "Leo," she said softly. Her enunciation of his name sounded like the distant peal of church bells, wind chimes dancing in the breeze, the twinkling songs of the stars.

"I am very sorry for your loss," she said with a tender squeeze of Heidi's shoulder.

Heidi felt a great wave of warm emotions surge from her belly and rise to flood her. Something like a bubble caught in her throat and she gulped. "Thank you," she said with a brave, wide smile. "I am sure I will find him soon. Until then, he makes his presence felt by his absence."

The witch scrunched up her brows. "Oh," she said, as her breath paused in mid-air. Confusion and concern creased her face. "So," she said at last, "I take it you are still looking for him?"

"Of course," Heidi replied promptly, careful to not let any tears spill from her eyes. "He will be thirteen soon. I will find him before that," she spoke with a conviction that had lodged into her with the arrival of Fuhen and his mistress, and grew stronger the longer she stayed with them and talked about looking for, and eventually, finding Leo.

Oh, she would find the right place alright, the one that Mr. Fox had alluded to. That would be the place where she will find Leo. She was getting closer, Heidi grew more and more certain.

"A-ha! A prime number!" the Oldest Witch sang out and waved an arm through the air. Snowflakes fluttered to her hand like tiny white birds. She caught them and promptly tossed them back out in the shape of numbers in dazzling white that twirled and whirled around Heidi.

Three stringed to a zero, and yet another zero, and a three again, followed by a seven, tailed by a six. More numbers followed, one tugging along the next gently, beads held together in a necklace by an invisible thread.

"The largest prime number thus far known to mankind," the Oldest Witch grinned. "Only over some twenty-two million digits long." Relief had settled once more on her face, as if she found herself back on familiar territory.

Another wave of her hand, and a new jumble of numbers wove and threaded through the air around them. "And this, the largest prime number discovered by yours truly. Running into well over a quadrillion digits," the Oldest Witch said grandly. She was beaming, her face lit up, happy, childlike.

But something in her appearance had changed at the same time. Tiny lines unexpectedly settled around her eyes and mouth. She snapped a finger and all the integers flew into her outstretched palms like birds hurrying back to their evening roosts. She pressed her fingers to her lips and blew a kiss to the cosmos. Tiny twinkling points of light soared heavenwards and lit up a sky inside her bubble.

Heidi gaped at the welkin with awe. "How many stars are there in the Universe?" she asked.

"I have a number for that too," the Oldest Witch smiled. "But it will take me an entire day and a half to read it out to you. Let us do something fun instead."

She pulled her personal sky closer and ran a finger from one star to another, joining the dots. The outline of a figure started to take shape. A hunter appeared. She quickly set to work on another image. A bear took shape.

The Oldest Witch's fingers were now gnarled, Heidi noticed. Knobbly and twisted, brittle branches of an old tree. Her robe hung limply on her frame, which was now slight and hunched, as if she had shrunk. Her hair was turning frail and wispy, and her face was furrowed with lines and shadows. The Oldest Witch was ageing.

Her skin was now softer, translucent, but happiness luminesced. The kind that came from having lived a life of purpose and meaning. She was an old star, glowing from within, playing in her own piece of sky.

But with each sleight of hand, time was taking its toll on her. It was requiring her to pay the price she had forgotten over the years. This was the price of having been incredibly young and extraordinarily beautiful once upon a time oh so long ago, and now she was being penalized for it.

But she continued to join the dots and gestured to Heidi to follow suit. Heidi, although not much of an artist, was unable to resist. She reached out to the stars and traced a hesitant image. Three inverted Vs, each progressively smaller, and a furl at the bottom.

A row of hills puffing out into the distance by the riverside. A half-sun beaming from behind them as if it were saying, *Peek-a-boo. Peak-a-boo. I see you.*

She turned to the Oldest Witch, her chest pounding with expectation.

"Serene," the Oldest Witch smiled. Her turn now. She traced what looked like a stick figure with a glowing head. A scarecrow. She pointed to the head and said, "That is Sirius, the brightest star in the night sky. And this constellation is …"

"Canis Major," Heidi chimed in. The Oldest Witch looked at her, impressed. A long, forgotten something stirred inside Heidi's mind. "The greater dog. Laelaps." Things she didn't know she knew unfurled inside her like an enlightenment. "And Sirius is the dog star."

An idea occurred to Heidi and she started to trace another image. Slowly, deliberately. Aiming for perfection in each stroke, each line. When she was done, she leaned back to check for flaws. Satisfied, she rubbed her shoulders and folded her arms tight across her chest. "There," she said proudly. "That is Leo."

"Handsome lad!" The Oldest Witch admired Heidi's work. She then frowned. "The numbers keep getting more and more startling. Did you know? No less than hundred dogs go missing every minute all across the world."

"And how many are found?" The words tumbled out of Heidi's mouth before she could stop them. "No," she hastily added. "No, please don't answer that. It doesn't matter. Because Leo will be found. I will find him," she shuddered a little with conviction and hugged herself even tighter.

The star shape of Leo came to life and bounded in that dream-filled sky. The Oldest Witch tugged at the heavens with both hands. And the sky fell upon them, a star-studded veil of gossamer. The snow-stars twirled and fell and settled around them like confetti.

The Oldest Witch folded the sable fabric and pressed it into Heidi's palm. "A piece of sky for you," the Oldest Witch said. "A special place. For you and Leo."

Heidi looked at the fabric in her palm. It was small and thin. Almost weightless, which was surprising for something that held the entire Universe within it. It felt like a piece of paper on which tiny hands had scrawled cryptic messages, a note inexplicably light for all the secret whispers and hushed giggles tucked within its folds and between its lines.

The hand that had presented her with the gift was once again slender and soft. No longer weighed down by illusions and starry desires, the Oldest Witch was young again.

"Why do you live in a bubble?" Heidi asked her.

"I have been around for longer than two dozen cosmic years, my dear," she smiled sadly. "I am older than the sun and the seas, and the moon and the mountains. They haven't aged a day. But you have seen me in my true form. Sometimes I like to go back to how everything used to be. How *I* used to be.

Young. Daring. Full of joy. And hope," she looked at Heidi. "Just like you."

She sighed. "And of course, there is the sticky issue of time. Too much time, in fact, so much that I don't quite know what to do with it all. So I concoct bubbles, of dreams and illusions, of hopes and desires, of promises and faith."

"But all bubbles burst eventually," Heidi said.

"And bring us back to reality, yes," admitted the Oldest Witch. "Which is where you need to head back to. So I must urge you to now go meet the Omniscient Man. Perhaps he can better guide you in your search for Leo."

She put an arm on Heidi's shoulder. Heidi once again felt safe and snug, as if she were inside a warm, protective cocoon of hope and belief.

"But Heidi, remember," the Oldest Witch said, a teacher instructing a child. "When you are on a quest, you will come across many things you weren't even looking for to begin with. Answers to questions you didn't ask. Solutions to conundrums that weren't yours to untangle. You will not always like what you come across. And what you want may not be yours to receive. You will have to learn to take all of this in stride. Eventually, you will have to learn to stop resisting. Teach yourself to accept what has happened in the past, and what is bound to come your way in the future. Let go of the past. Only then the way ahead will unfurl for you. Until then, you will find life has an annoying habit of becoming tediously repetitive."

The Oldest Witch then tugged at the leash and Fuhen stood up. The leash looked eerily familiar. A taut sash of brown against white fur and snow. Why did the Oldest Witch have Leo's leash? And Fuhen. Almost Leo. Where had he been all this while? With them, unmoving, frozen like a snow-dog?

"The leash," Heidi started, but the Oldest Witch and her dog were already wafting away from her. Backwards. Why were they gliding rather than walking?

"Hey, wait," she yelled but the distance between her and the Oldest Witch and Fuhen grew until she realized they were still standing at their spots. She was the one falling backwards, and fast. The bubble was receding rapidly.

It was as though she had jumped feet first into the ocean, and the sun overhead was furiously shrinking as she sank deeper and deeper until all light was blotted out.

Heidi held out a hand to stop the fall. She heard a growl. And then there was a blinding flash of white as a gaping maw snapped at her wrist. Terrified, she closed her eyes and screamed.

The back of her head hit a hard surface and for a moment she was straddling both her conscious and subconscious worlds, unable to tell one apart from the other. Her heart whomped violently against her chest.

When she opened her eyes, she found herself back on the outside of the white picket fence circling the sunlight-speckled glade that had held the Oldest Witch's snow globe only moments ago.

Now, tiny bubbles drifted innocently towards the evening sky. Delighted shrieks exploded in the air as the all too familiar tune of an ice cream truck filled the glade.

Heidi couldn't tell where the sounds were coming from. It all sounded like a childhood memory. Pushing and twisting its way through to the surface. Getting deformed along the way until she couldn't tell whether the happiness she associated with the scene was real or imagined.

Underneath all the tinkles and chimes was another sound that Heidi strained to hear. That of bubbles popping. The sound of air disappearing into air.

CHAPTER 3

A SWING, A WALK IN THE CLOUDS, AND THE OMNISCIENT MAN

Clouds hide the secrets of the skies from the prying eyes of earth dwellers, but they have a tendency to drift. So if one hangs about in the same spot for longer than an hour, as if lying in wait, it would be wise to stop and take notice of its unusual behaviour.

Which is what Heidi did. Which is why invisible hands lowered a swing from the cloud towards her. Heidi grabbed the ropes, hopped onto the swing, and pushed the ground away with her feet.

Back and forth, to and fro she swayed, the wind braiding her hair and spinning tornadoes in her viscera. With each oscillation, the swing lifted her higher and higher.

First, her feet kissed the treetops. The next thing she knew, the woods clinging to her backyard had shrunk so much she could blot them out with one foot. Leo, wherever he was, was now tinier than the smallest living cell in her body. Invisible to the naked eye.

Higher and higher she swung until she was in the clouds. Wet, misty tendrils whipped past her. The blue and green world below fell away and out of sight. All around, above and below her was a cold and grey domain of air and dew.

Here she was, weightless on the swing, and also crushed by the burden of Leo's absence. There was a sinking feeling in her soul, while she was also rising.

Here, in mid-flight, her face in the clouds, she had outgrown the world she had spent all her life in. And yet, somehow, in the vastness of the never-ending skies, she had also shrunk into nothing.

The dichotomy of her existence broke something inside of her. She threw back her head and laughed, the sound of it unexpected and unfamiliar to her own ears. The Pacific wind kissed her throat and tickled her in the spaces between her toes.

And then, easily and comfortably, as if she knew this was what she was meant to do all along, Heidi hopped off the swing. Hovering momentarily, she looked around. There it was, the rogue cloud, right above her. She flapped her hands as if they were wings and soared into the tufts of white nothingness.

An eternal moment later, she found herself in front of the Omniscient Man who was levitating above the snow-white cloud. He was smoking a pipe as long as his arm and chuffing out plumes of pearly smoke that spilled into the cloud and rolled away like little dust bunnies towards the setting sun.

Heidi dropped her arm-wings to her sides and walked towards him. Smoke whorled into the shape of Leo as she approached the Omniscient Man.

"He was a handsome one," he rasped. Leo-shaped clouds bounded about Heidi and gave her frenzied yaps before prancing away in caprioles. "The pipe reveals what you desire the most," he explained.

"Does it also reveal how I can obtain what I seek?"

The Omniscient Man studied his pipe closely, as if coaxing it to supply a suitable answer. Finally he said, "Not all desires are meant to be fulfilled, my child."

"Why are they thrown onto our path then, if they are not meant to come true?"

"So that in pursing them you will come across other desires, other dreams, those that are meant for you."

Panic seared her throat dry and garbled her words. "Does that mean … Are you saying … You think I may not … maybe I am not meant to find Leo?" she croaked.

She rubbed her fingers over her throat, but the warmth of skin on skin failed to soothe the rawness of fear. The thought she had so carefully fought to hide within her had now escaped her. Words had made it potent and it was out floating on the ether now, waiting to be reified.

She threw more words after it in a hasty attempt at retraction. "But I don't want other dreams. I was very happy and content where I was. And I want to go back there. All I want is to find Leo and go back home, and put all this behind me. Pretend all this was just an awful nightmare that never really happened," she pleaded.

The Omniscient Man smoked his pipe in a silence that clinked like tinnitus between Heidi's ears. He was older than the Oldest Witch, if that were possible. The skin on his face and hands creased into gentle folds and wrinkles, unable to stop growing even as his frail frame shrank with age.

A tailored suit topped with a Fedora hat held him together in the physical space his body occupied. His eyes, blue-grey marbles in a sea of white, globes of Earth in the vast universe, had seen and known everything.

"One way," he said, "to make peace with our sufferings is to look at that of others. A little perspective can go a long way." He stood up, surprisingly erect, and strode towards the setting sun. Heidi glided towards him, her arm-wings and legs somehow knowing how to move in harmony and propel her like a bird in lazy flight.

The Omniscient Man led her down an infinite path of white fluffy clouds underneath and blue sky all around and above them. As he walked, he puffed out a thick cloud from his pipe.

The smokescreen parted to reveal moving images of hundreds of fuggy soldiers wielding maces and swords and bows and arrows, charging at each other in a deafening clang of metal and bone.

The scene segued into another, one set in desolate valleys where nothing appeared to move but everything was obliterated by invisible hands wielding bombs and guns. The silence, when it came, was quieter than death.

Shrill cries of women and children next pierced the air around Heidi, as she witnessed fighter planes drop bombs on populated cities. Buildings and monuments and people exploded like badly designed fireworks that no one seemed to enjoy.

"War," said the Omniscient Man. "Uglier today than it was all those aeons ago."

He blew out another shroud of smoke. It smelled like incense and longing. The smoke curled into shapes of the dying and the dead from a bygone era, when doctors were rare and medicines even rarer. Then followed images of people dying of cancer and Alzheimer's, dying from a lifetime of breathing in adulterated air and wading through murky waters, an angry sun burning up their skin.

"Diseases, that not only ravage the body but also maim the mind, heart and spirit," the Omniscient Man said, as if reading the evening news off a teleprompter, his voice unmarred by emotion and inflection. Heidi felt sick to her stomach.

Yet another smokescreen. Rivers shrivelled up into narrow trickles of water. Trees withered into dead stumps. Lush mountains disintegrated into arid lumps of lifeless mud. Animals and birds gave up the ghost under a harsh, relentless sun.

"Our individual troubles pale in the face of the wounds festering in the heart of this beloved planet," the Omniscient Man said. "Sometimes, reminding ourselves of how small we are in the larger scheme of things could make our troubles shrink, if not disappear entirely."

He stood smoking his pipe while Heidi wondered what to say. She burnt with the desire to ask him where Leo was. She was certain he knew. He certainly knew more than she did. He was the Omniscient Man, the one who saw and knew everything.

But wouldn't it be impudent of her to pester him for details of her missing dog, an issue undoubtedly trivial in the face of all the historic developments he had to keep his eye on?

Before she could make up her mind, the Omniscient Man turned to her and said, "You have seen all that you needed to. I must take your leave now. The clouds will lead you to the light." And he walked back towards where they had come from, disappearing behind mists of smoke.

Heidi half-gilded, half-flew over the endless, white clouds towards the setting sun. A yellow sun, and a blue sky. Two primary colours. *A little bit of you and a little bit of me*, the sun seemed to be coaxing the skies. *Together, we concoct a palette of otherworldly hues and shades in the horizon.*

Heidi flapped her arm-wings. Closer and closer to the sun she flew. Her wings were made of burnished skin. They wouldn't melt. And the evening sun was tepid. All glow but no heat. Like dying embers in the grate.

Faster and faster, she flew. The sun was slipping over the edge of the sea of clouds.

"Wait," she called out. "Wait for me."

She was a human-bird, returning to an empty nest by the light of a falling star. She reached out to touch the face of the sun. As if moved by her gesture, the setting sun faltered.

And then, with renewed vigour, he rose from the occidental sky, casting a dragnet to draw back into him all the daylight that had been slipping away to make way for the night.

That is when Heidi saw the sun was not yellow. He never had been. His colour was white. It had always been.

White. A colour itself without hue. Yet, the colour of someone whose light reveals the myriad shades and tints of everything and everyone on the face of the earth. Like her, he too was conflicted.

He hurtled towards Heidi. His fire burned in the very centre of his being. She first felt his warmth. He dazzled her. She kept her eyes on him but he was too beautiful to look at without hurting, without crumbling within, without losing herself. Her eyes stung, and she squeezed them shut. She had all the light in the world to herself, yet she couldn't see a thing.

Tears spilled over but dried up under the sun's heat even before they could roll down her cheeks. It was as if she wasn't allowed to cry, because her grief was not lofty enough. As though her sorrow was a tiny grain of sand compared to the troubles of the cosmos.

Why then did it crush her chest with the weight of a thousand and one waves hurling themselves on an orphaned shore?

CHAPTER 4

LAUGHTER, THE HUNTSMAN, AND A RABBIT IN A WAISTCOAT

Heidi opened her eyes to find the tip of a grey, metallic arrow pressing down on her third eye.

She was lying on a surface that felt firm and hard underneath her. Bare earth, perhaps. Something tickled the nape of her neck. Blades of grass. Wildflowers.

Also she could see the sky above. Carmine, the kind that appeared only on the fringes of day and night.

Something gurgled and tumbled and whooshed past her incessantly. Water in motion. Wind bearing secrets to distant lands. Wings flapping. Her arm-wings. She had been too close to the sun, she recalled.

She stirred, and the tip of the arrow pressed down upon her. "I am harmless," she declared.

Now wasn't the time to risk injury or death. Not when Leo was waiting to be found. Yet the words tumbled out of her mouth before she had had a chance to consider them, "But I am not afraid to die."

Some newfound courage had taken root within and

pushed the words out of her, compelling her to take notice of them and acknowledge their veracity.

She took a deep breath, grabbed the arrow by its shaft and pushed it away from herself. She then rubbed her forehead where the weapon had dented her flesh.

A figure loomed into view. A thickset man. Sharp green eyes peered through a tangle of black and white hair that sprouted from his head and grew into his handlebar moustache and unkempt beard. He squinted into Heidi's face, then offered her his hand.

Pulling herself up, Heidi remarked, "So you've decided to spare my life?"

"I 'aven't yet made up my mind," the man said, his voice gravelly and rumbling as if from the bowels of the earth. "But I 'ave other prey to 'unt tonight. So let's just say yer ain't exactly on the top of my priority list. Especially, seeing as yer 'ave neither fangs nor claws," he explained.

He gingerly laid his bow and quiver of arrows on the ground, and dropped his sack next to it. The sight of his bag made Heidi wonder where her own was.

She looked around. To her right, maple trees, appareled in colours stolen from the earth and fire, burst forth like cinders against solemn pines. To her left gushed waters of different colours, blue as robin's eggs, cyanic as Uranus, and every hue that lay in between.

The hunter gathered a few dry twigs and started a fire. He produced a slain rabbit, skinned it expertly, and hung it over the fire to roast. He gathered a bunch of maple leaves and bent and twisted them, and then wove them into a water bowl that fit precisely in the palms of her hands.

"What brings yer to these parts of the woods?" he asked.

"Leo, my dog, is missing," Heidi said.

The huntsman was silent for a few moments. Heidi wondered if he already knew about Leo like all the others before him had.

"I'd like to say I am sorry. But I was bitten by a dog when I was a child. A German Shepherd it was. Beautiful beasts, but nasty when they turn on yer like that. That incident," he shuddered as if the mere recollection still terrified him after all these years, "isn't among the 'appiest of my childhood memories. So please excuse me if I'm not the most sympathetic to yer plight."

His words took Heidi by surprise and she didn't know how to respond. She wondered if she ought to take offence at his discourtesy or appreciate his undisguised candour.

The thought made her head spin. Thoughts about emotions. Thinking about how to feel. Like tasting which fragrance to smell. Or trying to see which sound to hear. The ridiculousness of it all made her laugh.

She threw her head back and laughed for a long time, and was relieved to find how easy it felt, how natural it was, because that was how she had wanted to respond to the huntsman. With laughter.

There was something so unassuming, so unpretentious in what he spoke that it seemed to lift a great weight off her chest. Air could once more travel in and out of her lungs, unrestricted, like wind through a flute. And she could breathe again. She could laugh again.

And it was a melody that came from her soul and floated away on the ether, carrying an essence of her over the river and through the maples and the pines. A song with wings.

Heidi doubled up with laughter. Her cheeks and jaw hurt.

A stitch tugged at her belly. She laughed so hard she could feel every cell in her body jiggle. Her skin tingled with the sensation. As if laughter was streaming out of every pore of her body.

Her skin was nothing but a net drawn through the air to keep her flesh and bones intact, but now all the emotions that made Heidi who she was were spinning out of her, like autumn foliage being blown away by the wind to clear the path for something else, and she was dissolving in the deluge. At long last, the girl had become the laughter, the singer had become the song.

When silence finally wrapped itself around her, she sat and stared into the distance for a long time, a different person than she had been moments ago. The huntsman sat quietly next to her, partaking of his meal, patience not a stranger to him.

When the time came, Heidi turned to him and confessed, "I suppose I'd feel that way too if someone were to lose their pet snake. I am not at all a fan of anything that creeps, crawls or slithers."

The huntsman nodded. "I 'ear yer," he said. Pieces of meat clung to his beard. He licked his fingers clean and rose to wash himself in the waters.

Heidi waited for the question that never came. About her momentary plunge into insanity. For an instant she was gripped with the urge to talk, to explain, more to herself than to him, how his candour had unravelled something in her but had also infused her with hope.

A few words uttered by him, without any pretence or chimera, had given her a level of acceptance about her situation that had nothing to do with bubbles and illusions, or smoke and mirrors.

Her loss may be small, irrelevant even, in the face of world-changing events and happenings, but Leo was, had always been, and will always be a significant part of her world, and she an immense presence in his. He was counting on her to come to his rescue. This was his hour of need and she was the sole person who could track him down and bring him back home.

Heidi was suddenly furious with the Oldest Witch and the Omniscient Man for having left her devoid of belief and conviction when what she needed most was faith and hope. The ones who had embraced life for the longest were the ones who had lost faith in it, she realized.

Heidi had an inkling of a desire to share all her thoughts with the huntsman. She was as excited with her realization as Archimedes must have been when he stepped into that life-altering bath. This was her Eureka moment.

But the silence that had settled in her was some sort of a magic spell she didn't want to ruin with the sound of too many words and the noise of their meanings and misapprehensions.

Besides, these were her truths to discover, to stumble upon. It would be foolish to expect another to perceive her truth in exactly the same fashion as she did. It would, no doubt, be distorted in translation.

"Thank you," she said. "For your truth," she added, satisfied with her choice of words.

The huntsman nodded. He doused the fire, gathered his sack and weapons, and rose. "Where will yer go from 'ere?" he asked.

"I don't know," Heidi answered. Come to think of it, she had so far not given much thought to where she was headed. Finding Leo was her sole mission but she had been going about it with no plan or strategy, merely coasting along hoping to find someone or something that would yield her a clue as to Leo's whereabouts.

The trouble was she seemed to be going places without any recollection of her arrivals and departures. "What about yourself?" she asked.

"I am looking for the Red Fox," he revealed. "'Ave you seen him?"

"Not a red one. But a silver fox," she said, remembering her encounter the first night she ventured into the woods.

"When? Where?" the huntsman asked. His eyebrows were raised and reminded Heidi of how Leo would perk up his ears at something that merited attention.

"A long time ago, in a faraway place, of which I know little else and where I am sure he no longer is," Heidi replied, truthfully.

"I don't blame yer," he shook his head. "Red. Silver. Them's all the same. Slippery one that red beast is. Took 'alf my coop, 'e did. Led them out like the Pied Piper. Yer should 'ave seen them 'ens, cackling and falling over themselves as they followed 'im into these woods. Like a bunch of old 'ags gone gaga over a young dandy. Tch!"

He ground the toecap of his boot into the earth, as if stubbing out an invisible cigarette. "Well," he sighed, "I better be off." He pointed to the grass beside her. Chunks of roasted meat lay untouched in her bowl. "Let the rabbit not 'ave been slain in vain," he said, and marched off into the thicket of pines and maples. The earth under Heidi shuddered.

She reached out to the bowl next to her when a sudden gust of wind blew it away and turned it upside down. Heidi got up and picked up the bowl. A streak of white darted out from underneath it and hopped up and down in front of her. Heidi screamed.

It was a large, white rabbit with pink ears and long whiskers. It was wearing a waistcoat and pulled out a watch. "Hurry," it squeaked and hopped away towards the trees. It turned back to see Heidi still rooted to her spot, and came hopping back towards her. It pulled her by her leg. "Hurry, or we'll be late."

Heidi let herself be dragged along, half-amused, half-intrigued by this ankle-high ball of fluff bumbling across the grass and into the trees. "Where are we going?" she asked.

"There," the rabbit pointed to a maple tree that had a tiny hollow at its base. The hole was just large enough for Heidi to push a fist through, where it was likely to remain for eternity.

As they approached the tree, the hole grew larger and larger. A door swung open. A door? The rabbit leaped across the threshold. Heidi jumped into the hollow after him.

Down the rabbit hole she fell. The light receded, taking with it the woods and the water, the huntsman and the bowl of maple leaves, and her laughter that bore the message, *Heidi was here*.

She tried to capture everything in a memory, a snapshot in her mind for keepsake, but it had all disappeared into the darkness long before she could realize what she was leaving behind.

Like a dream scurrying into her subconscious so she wouldn't carry it into the waking world where it didn't belong.

CHAPTER 5

A WALL, A JOINT, AND THE BOY

A wall of red and grey stones rose from the ground and reached for the skies. It ran endlessly to her right and to her left, as far as Heidi could see.

She had always thought it was the woods that stretched from her backyard all the way until the end of the world, where land, water and sky greeted each other all at once.

But now the wall, an endless cluster of stones piled one atop the other, seemed to demarcate a boundary. Some sort of before and after. Something that would change her irreversibly should she cross over to the other side. Like a first kiss. Or a heartbreak. Or the death of a loved one.

A shadow stirred, and a tall, pale figure emerged from the wall. A young man, a boy perhaps, appeared and leaned easily with one foot up against the wall. He pulled a joint from behind his ear and lit it up. He smoked unhurriedly. Time waited for him to indulge in his vice.

"What's on the other side?" asked Heidi.

"Depends," the boy shrugged, "What you want, where you want to go."

"I am looking for my dog, Leo," Heidi replied. "He's gone missing. I want to find out what has become of him."

The boy dragged on his reefer. His eyes glazed over and Heidi got the sense he wasn't entirely with her. Left foot pressed against the wall, left hand in his pocket, his joint pressed between the thumb and forefinger of his right hand. Tendrils of copper- and brass-coloured hair coiled atop his head like a bird's nest, a vestige of his boyhood. A private joke he was apparently trying hard to keep secret was teasing its way out of his mouth through a lopsided grin.

In another time, in another place, Heidi would have had a crush on him. In this time, in this place, she wanted to give him a proper snog.

As soon as the thought planted itself in her mind, she mentally chastised herself. She hadn't come this far in her search for Leo only to be led astray now by amorous urges for a stranger.

"Meet Starburst," he drawled. Something rustled and stirred in his rusty locks, then bolted out like a flash of blue and white lightning. A pair of wings flapped against Heidi's face. The laughter of a madman exploded in her ears and knocked her off her feet. Thrown to her back on the ground, shellshocked, Heidi saw it for what it was. Blue-winged and spangle-faced. A kookaburra. Higher and higher it flew, circling the world, a tiny speck of bird in the sky, its laughter crazed and ear-splitting, rattling the wind wherever it went.

Heidi sat up with half a mind to give Starburst and his owner a piece of her mind. But at that very instant the boy dropped easily on to the ground beside her, and gave her that lopsided grin that overruled everything else. "Here, this should help," he said, holding out the joint he had been smoking. Or had he been rolling a new one when the bird was going crazy?

Heidi closed her eyes and took a deep drag. Smoke soaked through her lungs and veins. She puckered her lips, and puffed out trembling rings of sweet smelling smoke. The kookaburra hollered somewhere in the distance. "Starburst, indeed!" she snorted.

"Come," the boy held out a hand. "Something I'd like you to see."

Heidi looked into his eyes, soft and brown like Leo's, and fancied she could look into them for a lifetime. She glanced at his outstretched arm, an invitation she wanted to grab without further thought. She turned her gaze to the joint in her hand. It was like a magic wand that had somehow slowed down time. Smoke in. Smoke out.

Starburst laughed somewhere far over their heads. Happiness bubbled from deep within her and Heidi laughed merrily, her voice sounding sweet and mellifluous to her own ears. She wondered what the boy thought.

She slipped her hand into his, and he closed his fingers around hers. She was a pearl, safe and snug, tucked inside an oyster. The world around her quivered ever so gently, a ripple on the face of water.

Heidi stood up and everything swam around her in a placid, fluid motion. The wall loomed above her like a large piece of harlequin fabric, red and grey, undulating like a scarf in the breeze. The ground on which she stood swayed, a large magic carpet in flight.

She stretched out her hands and tried to find her balance but kept tumbling into the boy. "Sorry," she giggled, "I think I was born a plane, and then I somehow became human. But

I still need to spread my wings. Else I will fall," she blabbered.

"Pretty sure Starburst saw you for what you were," the boy grinned. "A plane. No wonder the sight of you sent him skittering through the skies." Heidi put a hand over her mouth to suppress her giggles and failed miserably.

The boy led her to a flight of narrow, rickety steps that crept up the wall.

"Shhh!" he put a finger to her lips. "Think the wind can hear us," he whispered mock-conspiratorially in her ear.

That sent Heidi into another bout of uncontrollable laughter. "The wind … she loves you. Look, she is trying to blow me away," she sang out and pretended to fall backward. Bodies bumbling, knees scraping, elbows jostling, words garbling, limbs interlinking, laughter mingling, they went up the stairs.

So much commotion when she could barely feel her body anymore, Heidi thought. She felt light as a feather, weightless as a snowflake. She looked down and was delighted to find her shoes barely grazed the ground anymore. "Look, I am a plane again," she cooed excitedly. "Ready to take off anytime now."

"Here," the boy replied, "At your runway now."

Somehow they had managed to bob and bounce up the stairs without falling right back down or lifting up and floating away. And they were now standing on top of the wall. Only, it wasn't her wall anymore.

What had been a pile of stones barely a few feet tall now towered over a vast city of green and concrete so far below she wondered how high they were. Twinkling points of light glittered and shimmered everywhere she looked, as if the city was illuminated for one giant celebration. Behind her the waves of a blue ocean gently caressed an endless shore over and over again as if they had nowhere else to go, nothing else to do. The lights of travelling ships blinked from a reverential distance.

Above, the sky was mostly pale, blue disappearing into white. There was no sun. But on one end, the wall ran into a pool of nameless colours splashed lazily over the blue-whiteness. As if colours had spilled from a palette and someone had done a very slipshod job of mopping them up.

Heidi couldn't quite tell if it was dawn or dusk. If the day was ending or another was beginning. If they were on land or in air. Or on water.

She couldn't see the base of the wall anymore. They were in some in-between time and place. As if she were walking on the edge of a precipice. Or on the horizon. On a tightrope stretched taut between life and death.

As though time didn't want to stir from this place, and all the three dimensions of space had collapsed into this singular moment.

The darkness arrived eventually. But it did so in the blink of an eye. As if someone had flung a sable blanket over the world. It brought with it the moon and the stars, and their light. Land, water, and air all became indistinguishable forms of blackness. But all the lights in the three regions burned more ferociously, brighter against the tenebrosity of the world.

"Ready to take off?" the boy said, his voice settling slowly and gently into the stillness around her. He dragged on his spliff and the burning end glowed and waned to the rhythm of soft crepitations.

It was beautiful. Serene. Like the rise and fall of her chest with every breath in and every breath out. A smile tugged at her lips and a tranquil joy pressed upon her cheeks. Her heart content, her mind wandered to his question.

"Where will I go?" she wondered matter-of-factly, as if it were a philosophical question to ponder over at leisure.

"In search of Leo," the boy reminded her.

Heidi nodded, pleased he had been paying attention to her. The world around her glowed a little more brightly. There was so much light surely some of it would have fallen on to Leo's path, Heidi assured herself. Even if he were not with her, he was safe and warm somewhere, just as she was now. They were not together but they were still under the same ebon sky, in the company of strangers, watching the lights and shadows shift and play. Perhaps there was no need for her to rush after him. She could take a little longer, bask in this forgotten happiness for some more time.

And so she said, "But I haven't the slightest clue where he is." For now, that excuse was good enough to stall for time, to hang on to this moment of happiness and draw it out until eternity. It was also true enough to stave off any feelings of guilt.

The boy looked at her and spoke his first full sentence with deliberate grammatical accuracy. "Often we know more than we think we do. We must bring ourselves to see, and acknowledge, what lies right in front of our very eyes, hollering for our attention this very instant before we go seeking in other lands."

The boy's words stupefied Heidi. Standing on top of the world, dragging on a spliff, blowing out sweet smoke and unexpected words of wisdom, he looked like God's gift to her, an unexpected answer to all the questions she hadn't even thought to ask. 42!

She threw back her head and laughed. The kookaburra called from another world in response. "Then let me begin with what lies right in front of my very eyes, hollering for my attention this very instant," she giggled.

She stepped close to him and placed a hand on his chest. His heart beat against her palm and sent little flutters up her arm and down to her chest. The easy, rhythmic trot of an unhurried horse. Her breath fell into step.

She stood on tiptoe and kissed him. Briefly, at first. But without hesitation. She then drew back and imagined herself reflected in his honey eyes. Happiness rose in her cheeks and her heart sang.

The boy smiled and put his arms around her waist. She slid her arms around his neck. And they closed their eyes and kissed for a long, long time.

Two souls searching for each other, past the physical barrier of skin, under the argent faux-light of the moon. Lovers from a forgotten aeon crossing paths in this lifetime for a fleeting glimpse of each other before they went their own ways once more.

Dawn was breaking over the wall and chasing the darkness away from the skies, the ocean, and the land when they finally came up for air.

"I feel as if I have indulged in all the goodness that life had to offer," Heidi said. "Thanks to you," she added.

The boy ruffled her hair and gave her his lopsided smile. Heidi thought it would break her heart to bid farewell but to her own surprise she was content enough to leave. Everything that needed to be said and done had been said and done.

Lingering around would only provoke needless conversations and deeds. Before she had a chance to doubt her certainty, she said, "It is time for me to leave."

The boy dragged on his reefer, which had burnt down right to the end and Heidi wondered if it would burn his lips. He then flicked it into the distance. It flew over the wall and fell into the mosaic of brown and green and grey quadrangles, gently twirling and disappearing like a thread in a fabric.

He looked at her and shrugged. "Ready to take off?" he asked. Heidi nodded, then spread her arms and calmly stepped over the edge of the wall, falling face down towards the hard, unyielding terrain of dry land.

CHAPTER 6

AN ACCIDENT, A DEAD LEO, AND THE FURY OF GAIA

Heidi cupped her palms over her eyes and rubbed her temples with her thumbs, but the pounding from within refused to subside.

Her throat was parched and her lips were dry. She ran her tongue over her lips and swallowed. It hurt. A faint whiff of something odd swirled around her, something like stale smoke that might have been intoxicating once upon a time.

She rubbed her face and head and opened her eyes to the blinding light of a hot summer afternoon on a vast, grassy flatland that sprawled towards infinity on all sides.

A hidden sound whooshed all around her. An incessant rushing, like that of motor vehicles on a highway, or waves on the shore. She couldn't tell where it came from or where it was going. The endlessness of it frayed her nerves.

Heidi shaded her eyes and scanned the horizon for an exception to the bleak panorama. A route. A destination. A way out of here. The sight of the desolate landscape exhausted her. The sun beat hard upon the earth, all the stars having been outshone into oblivion.

Tired and thirsty, she was now also annoyed with herself for having landed in the middle of nowhere. She must have dropped from the skies, she reckoned, seeing as there was no other way she could have arrived here.

She looked around once more. Somewhere in the distance, beyond the corner of her eye, a tiny structure shimmered. She half-walked, half-ran towards it. It appeared to move towards her too, growing larger and larger.

A chimney stuck out at the top like a middle finger. Plumes of rusty brown smoke puffed out and squatted over what had now taken the shape of a farmhouse with a barn next to it. White specks, like land-stars, dazzled on the surrounding grounds. Heidi picked up pace. She tried not to blink lest her destination disappear like a mirage.

As she approached the farmhouse, the world took on a monochromatic hue. Sepia-toned. The colour of dry earth. The shade of dust. Blades of grass, as brown as dry twigs, rustled in the hot breeze.

Grazing contentedly on the fields were white baby unicorns, white as little lambs, their petite horns whorling like auger shells. They were under the protective eyes of two brown and white border collies that bounded towards Heidi as soon as she set foot on the muddy hazel path that led up to the farmhouse.

One had eyes so intensely blue Heidi knew its colour was stolen from the sky. She looked up and saw that the heavens were a pallid beige, as if burnt by the raging heat of the sun. The other had eyes as purple as verbena as if to counterpoise with the infertile colourlessness of this part of the world.

The two dogs flanked Heidi as she made her way towards the house, walking right in the centre of the path, keeping her distance from their panting tongues and bared teeth. She knew better than to caress them.

Small pools of turbid water speckled the path leading to the house, souvenirs of a long ago rainfall in this scorched land, shining gold on the muddy earth. Red bricks, long faded to a tawny colour, piled atop each other and held up the house under a straw roof. The barn, a shambling frame of thatched mat and bamboo sticks, stood behind and away. A rusty tractor, having lost its wheels, rested immobile next to it.

A woman was leaning against it, her skin stippled and her hair dry and bleached like a bale of hay. She looked like she was made of earth but, like the tractor, had corroded and worn out over time.

She was Gaia, named after the earth, Heidi knew somehow, and that was just as well for no introductions were forthcoming.

"I once had a collie named Leo," Gaia said. "A very long time ago."

"What happened to him?" Heidi asked.

"He died," Gaia said. Her voice was so devoid of emotion it made Heidi shudder. "A car ran him over. One of those that you folk drive at breakneck speeds. Only you break others' necks, not your own."

A faraway look came into her eyes, as if she were peering into a very distant past. "It happened right there," she pointed in the general direction of the muddy path Heidi had walked on, and snapped her fingers.

As if on cue, colours sneaked up from wherever they were hiding behind the edges of the world and drenched every pixel of the dreamscape. Lush green grass pushed up from the earth on which they stood and sparkled with silver dew.

Behind Gaia, the farmhouse and the barn shimmered back to life, gleaming a warm brownish-red. Golden crops of wheat sprung up in the farmland behind the house and swayed to a gentle breeze. In front, the dirt path that had led Heidi to the house disappeared under a sheet of gravel. The fields beyond transformed into endless rivers of lavender racing with the azure blue skies to kiss the horizon. A road of tar and chip unfurled between the grassy expanse and the lavender fields like a strip of ribbon tied around a gift box. Only the unicorns remained white, dazzling whiter now against the backdrop of colour.

Gaia, now resuscitated with the gift of colour and joy, sat on the grass, a baby unicorn ensconced on her lap. Her dress swirled around them in a maze of blue and green, the colours of a dancing peacock.

Leo, Gaia's Leo, stood at the end of the gravel path, barking at another little unicorn that had strayed into the lavender fields across the road, urging the errant baby to come back. The unicorn pranced and frolicked about in the fields, dancing to an inaudible tune. A silver star on its forehead threw an occasional twinkle their way as it turned and caught the light of the sun.

Trucks and wagons carrying bales of hay and corn trundled by on the chip-sealed road. An occasional car sped past. Leo looked to the right, then to the left, then bounded across the road when the coast was clear and caught up with the unicorn.

The two frolicked around each other, nudging and nuzzling playfully. A skip to the left, a leap to the right, then the unicorn rose in a capriole, then made an unexpected dart across the road for home.

A blotch of red shot into the road from thin air. Leo rushed after the horned-horse, put his nose to the baby's rear and flung him into the air and across the road, straight into the safety of Gaia's arms.

All eyes were on the injured foal. No one saw Leo disappear under the mass of red that sped past. A messy pool of carmine flesh and shattered bones on the road were all that remained of him.

In that world of colours, Gaia flung herself on the sanguinary remains of her beloved collie. Sobs and moans racked her body so hard Heidi thought the distressed woman would fall apart into pieces. A rage-filled caterwaul erupted from the depths of Gaia's soul and splintered the air around them. Flames roared in her eyes and an invisible fire scorched every inch of land and sky within her sight.

"Earth to earth," Gaia snapped, as the colours receded faster than they had appeared. Her anger singed the world that was now simmering in the heat that seemed to have settled there permanently.

Heidi stood in silence. She opened her mouth a little to say something but decided that nothing was appropriate and shut it again. She stood motionless, not knowing what to do, afraid to disturb the stillness that was pressing upon them like a snug blanket that was too heavy and warm for comfort.

"Go," Gaia made the decision for her. "Leave now. And never come back," she hissed. Her face was so contorted with rage and grief Heidi looked away, terrified. She scurried down the muddy path and when she thought it wouldn't be impolite, broke into a run without a backward glance. A door slammed somewhere behind her and the baked ground beneath her juddered. For the first time since she had set out in search of Leo, Heidi wondered if he was still alive.

Hot, angry tears rolled down her cheeks and mingled with sweat and snot as she ran towards nowhere in particular.

She tried not to think that Leo, her Leo, was quite possibly dead. The image of Gaia's dog as a bloody mess abandoned on the streets wouldn't leave her mind.

Heidi willed herself to focus on the rhythmic thump of her sneakered feet on the hard ground. Her heart pounded in sync. A cacophony of emotions grated her nerves.

The likelihood that Leo was no more did not frighten her as much as it angered her. How could he be dead after all the effort she had put in to look for him? It was so unfair, so bloody unfair. And then she cursed herself for having used the word 'bloody'.

She stomped on the pavement harder so as to drown the voices in her head but her mind raced on. Surely Leo wasn't dead? But how could she be sure?

She had been wandering for days, aimlessly now it seemed, as if she'd been stuck in a dream, stumbling into whimsical characters with outlandish notions of life and death and everything in between, and she wasn't any closer to finding out what had become of Leo.

And if he was dead and gone, where was she headed now? What was she running towards? Or was there something she was running away from?

Heidi ran towards the nearest tree and slammed her fists into its trunk. The physical impact allowed some of her fury to dissipate. It released some of the rage that would have otherwise fulminated within and annihilated her.

Relief followed. All the collywobbles that had been

mutilating her mind disappeared and a warm sense of relief and peace settled over her from head to toe like new skin.

Breathing evenly, she looked around and found she was back in the land of green maples and pines. A chipsealed road snaked through the green expanse under a clear, blue sky. Behind her, Gaia's world of burnt sepia was only a few steps away, separated by an invisible, undulating film of hot air rising from the parched earth.

Now that she was safely away from the fury of a bereaved soul, Heidi felt a twinge of pity for Gaia rise in her heart. But she quickly made up her mind to not dwell on the tragic fate of the dead dog but to focus instead on finding her missing but hopefully alive one. Not wanting to waste any more time, she turned away from the wall and decided to explore the new terrain that surrounded her.

The Universe obviously had other plans in mind for Heidi, for it promptly sent her way a red car that appeared on the road unannounced and crept towards the invisible palisade, the driver perhaps expecting the car to run into the wall. And it did. He pressed down on the accelerator and the engine rumbled insistently and louder. The wheels bore furious pits into the ground splattering mud and grit all over the car but the invisible barrier did not budge.

The driver gave up at last. He switched off the engine and stepped out of the car. No act of frustration. No thwacking of the steering wheel with his hands. No slamming of the door. No cursing as he looked down to confirm what he already knew; the car had sunk a few inches into the ground.

He turned to Heidi, shook his head and smiled sadly. "Looks like Gaia is still burning with rage," he said.

Heidi looked at him, and his flashy red car, and a thought crossed her mind. "It was you, wasn't it?"

He nodded.

"And not a day has since gone by when I've not cursed myself for the terrible crime, but …" he stopped abruptly, then opened his mouth to speak some more. But the words remained lodged in his throat. As a matter of habit, Heidi thought. Whatever the man had wanted to share had been suppressed for far too long and was not yet ready to be revealed.

"But?" Heidi encouraged.

"I come here every year on the day it happened," he said, and Heidi knew he wasn't picking up from where he had left off. "To seek her forgiveness. To placate her. Every year I turn back from this very spot, unable to step over to the other side of her grief."

It struck Heidi that there was something oddly familiar about the man. She was almost certain they had met before but further detail eluded her.

His was the kind of persona you could forget in the blink of an eye. Ordinary face, ageless almost, she couldn't tell how old he was. Blue jeans, white tee with a faded print on the front, black jacket, and white and red sneakers. Nothing that stood out and screamed, "Remember me!" He was utterly forgettable. She wondered if this was by design.

Yet she strongly suspected this wasn't their first encounter. They had met before. But whether in an earlier lifetime or in a dream, she couldn't recall.

She walked over to the invisible wall and, despite her earlier misgivings, extended a tentative toe on to the brown land on the other side. She could still cross the boundary that kept him out.

She turned back and held out a hand to the man. He clasped her outstretched fingers and she pulled him. He walked face first into the wall and fell back like a boxer rebounding off the ropes back into the centre of the ring.

"This year is no different," he said, rubbing the back of his neck and shaking his head sadly. He looked up at Heidi straddling the unspoken boundary with apparent ease, and something between embarrassment and irritation flashed across his face.

"Gaia behaves as if hers is the only loss that matters," he grumbled. The forbidden words had found their release at last. But the very next instant he squeezed his eyes shut and pinched the bridge of his nose as if he already regretted the words that had irreversibly spilled out of his mouth.

Heidi could see him struggle with his emotions as they warred with his notion of right and wrong. All the same, she snapped, "Why shouldn't she?" She felt the stirrings of a recently subsided fury well up within her again. A tiny part somewhere deep inside held her back. For now, at least.

The man looked at her in surprise. "Because after a while that loss, that grief will be the only thing that will matter. You have to learn to let go. If you hold on to it for too long, it will start holding you back, and everything else will wither away. All that pain, all that rage, it will only grow and grow until there is no space left in you for anything else. No space for happiness. No room for joy. None whatsoever for love. For life."

His use of the second-person pronoun did not go unnoticed by Heidi. She momentarily wondered if it was a deliberate choice or a slip of the tongue. She shelved the thought and drew her mind back to what the man had just said about loss and its attendant grief overriding every other feeling and emotion.

What was she feeling about Leo's absence? As if in response, the dark, inexplicable emotions that had taken root in her without her knowing, without her consent, at some time when she was in Gaia's land, resumed their clamour for attention.

Heidi wanted to take all her shapeless, formless emotions and render them tactile, tangible. Her grief and pain, her loss and sorrow, all these were abstract concepts that she could not quite explain in words and no one else would ever comprehend them in their entirety.

In this physical world, she needed somatic manifestations of all the invisible wounds on her soul. She needed to transform them into scars on her body, souvenirs of a pain that she could later see and touch and kiss to remind herself how profound her grief had been, how overwhelming her loss had been.

Blood roared in her ears with the force of a relentless avalanche. The space between and around her temples buzzed with an electric energy so strong and unbridled she knew not what to do with it.

She had a sudden urge to expend this abrupt burst of power. Kick the car. A few thwacks on the back and sides of her skull. Pummel her fists into a tree. Slap her cheeks till they turned red and raw.

The physical impact would melt her emotions into something soothing, like a warm bath or a snug blanket. And then she would feel fine. Relieved. Drained of energy but also lighter because of it.

But she didn't want witnesses to her newfound madness. So she clenched her fists and hoped that would suffice for now. She imagined ramming a fist into her own mouth, splitting a lip, knocking off some teeth. She could almost taste the warm, metallic tang of blood in her bruised mouth. The thought helped take the edge off the violence of all the unnamed emotions that racked her soul.

When she spoke, it was with a calmness that belied her internal turmoil and sounded strange and alien to her own ears. "Gaia will never forgive you. And so you have concocted this balderdash. For what? So that you can live with yourself. It is all very well for you to say we have to let go of our grief and rage. But who are you to dictate to us how we should or shouldn't feel? When we ourselves don't quite know what to make of this onslaught of emotions and thoughts?"

And Heidi knew she was no longer talking about Gaia, but about herself. Tears spilled over her wide, open eyes. The tight, intense knot of sentiments that had been eating away at her insides burst open and ran down her cheeks like pent-up waters bursting through a broken dam. And alongside ran shame and guilt, for feeling the things she felt, and for how intensely she felt them, not quite knowing why.

When she was able to catch her breath between tears, she whispered, "But I hope you are right," she told the man. "About the need to let go. I only hope I can learn to."

She was spent. She couldn't comprehend how Gaia had the strength to keep smouldering, day after day, year after year, without crumbling into cinders. She shivered a little.

"You will know," the man assured her. "You will know when it's time."

He walked towards his car. Heidi watched him. Another strange character, she thought. Perhaps not as outlandish as the others that had come her way before him. But like all the others, he too carried with him the onus of his story. One that she felt compelled to listen to and understand before she could resume her quest.

What did all these stories mean? What did they tell her about those who were unburdening themselves, revealing their oldest, deepest secrets to her?

The Oldest Witch in her big bubble of denial. And her penchant for numbers. What digits will she assign to the emotions that were now turning Heidi inside out? Zero? Infinity was more like it.

The Omniscient Man who had spoken with eloquence about the sorrows of the world. Who, for all his knowledge and wisdom, could comprehend nothing at all of her grief.

The Huntsman, so awkward in his commiserations. Laughter bubbled out of Heidi once more at the memory of her encounter with him.

And then the Boy. A warm blush rose up her neck and cheeks at the thought of him. All that joy now rattled by her encounter with Gaia.

It occurred to Heidi that the sobriquets of some of these characters sounded like the titles of tarot cards. The face cards or the major arcana. Put together, were they about to reveal her future, she wondered.

And, oh! She had nearly forgotten Mr. Fox. The very first being she had met on her journey through the woods. What had he said? That the right place would be the one where she finds Leo. Until then, every place would feel wrong. Very wrong.

Maybe that is what all these characters were. Wrong places she had to pass by so as to get to the right one.

What about this man in the car then? Was he a wrong turn too? A regular bloke trying to mediate between her warring selves. Telling her to make peace before it was too late. But was it already too late?

Somewhere in the not too distant past she had splintered into different fragments, each guided by a different emotion, each tugging at her heart and pulling her in a different direction. No matter which route she chose, she wouldn't arrive at her destination whole. Only a broken piece of her would persist till the end, the other fragments refusing to tag along in disagreement. She realized she would have to choose which way to go. Choose which fragments to keep, which ones to discard.

The immensity of the decisions that lay in front of her terrified her. She wasn't ready yet, she told herself. Perhaps a little more time, a little more thought would provide a little more clarity. The man had said she would know when the time came. Now, the present moment, didn't feel like the right time for such a momentous task. She ought to keep going towards Leo. But how many more of these odd bods was she going to encounter before she ran into him? Was she ever going to find him? Now that she had permitted herself this crack of a doubt, it kept haunting her. Like an unanswered question, an unsolved query, a deep conundrum. Like one of those scientific problems that remained unsolved for generations.

Heidi jumped when the man started his car. Seeing him

about to depart, she remembered one more thing. "Wait," she called. "You look so familiar ... I wondered ... Have we met before?"

The man rolled down the window on his side and smiled. "Of course we will meet again," he shouted back over the roar of the engine. And the car disappeared like a flash of red.

CHAPTER 7

THE SECRET OF THE DREAM PEDLAR

There is a man who sells dreams for a living.

Dreams of all sensations and durations.

Dreams that take your breath away.

Fantasies that thrill and overwhelm. Illusions that leave you spellbound.

Reveries for the noontime. Will-o'-the-wisps for the witching hour.

Chimera that last barely a few breaths. Flights of fancies that never end.

Age-old dreams that were dreamt into existence by the Gods themselves. Some others as pristine as a newborn. A few rare ones yet undreamt of.

"Come hither, my dearies," the man calls, "for your dream-rides."

But no two dreams are alike. To choose one, you must let go of the rest. Ah, choices! You have countless dreams to pick from, but only one can truly be yours today.

If you ask him where the dreams come from, he will demur.

But I know.

I have seen him slip through the cracks between the worlds, slither from the light to the shadows, and knock on the doors of the ghosts of the living dead.

They don't let him in. They open their windows instead and throw out dreams they wish to discard, desires they could do without, like irresponsible residents littering their neighbours' alleyways.

The man gathers all the discarded dreams and loads them on to his cart. He then trundles back to his cave where he sorts and tags and places them in boxes and bottles and baubles and wraps them up in muslin and glitter and ribbons, and loads them on to his cart once more and makes his way to where you wander, trying to keep yourself from getting lost.

And he sells you these broken dreams for less than a ha'penny because he knows, whether you know it or not, that only you can mend them.

CHAPTER 8

A TELEPHONE CALL, A LULLABY, AND MOTHER

Fairy lights held up high, sloping eaves. Flaming torches set in sconces on the walls made shadows dance all around the room.

More people than Heidi had ever run into in her long life of seventeen years milled about in a room that was larger than her house back in the village, clinking glasses filled with liquids of psychedelic colours. Not one face was familiar. Everybody was talking and laughing at the same time, it seemed, and Heidi wondered if that was even possible.

She was alone, the only one by herself in the room. She squeezed her way past groups of people, occasionally nodding and smiling at everyone in general and at no one in particular, while trying to avoid being elbowed by those whose entire bodies were engaged in animated conversations.

She was looking for someone. Someone who should have turned up several moons ago.

A different someone thrust a dainty flute of steaming, silver liquid in her hand. She threw back her head and quaffed the drink. Her throat felt hot and cold at the same time as if a cool breeze were wiping the hot sweat off her brow.

A tap on her shoulder. A guy with Leo's eyes. Oval-shaped, honey-coloured. Wet and full of wonder.

"Your mum's on the line," he said and jerked a thumb over his shoulder. Behind him and several other people was an archway with the word *Telephone* engraved into the wall above it, flanked by two flaming torches.

The room was no larger than a telephone booth. The instant Heidi stepped through the doorway, the noise of the party fell away.

An instrument, the likes of which Heidi had only seen in black-and-white movies, sat atop a small table. The receiver lay in its cradle.

Heidi looked behind for the Leo-eyed messenger but he had disappeared into the crowd.

She turned back and lifted the receiver to her ear.

The cracked, faraway strains of a familiar tune played in the distance on the other end. A lullaby. The one that her mother used to sing to her every night.

"Mumma?" she whispered, suddenly afraid there would be no response.

"Oh my baby, my baby!" The sound of her mother's gentle voice was all the permission Heidi needed, and she broke down and sobbed like a child.

"My dear, dear child," her mum said, over and over again. Her voice was soft and kind and wrapped itself around Heidi like a warm blanket over her shoulders as if to say, *You are in a safe place now, it is alright to grieve here.*

And so Heidi cried and cried. For Leo. For her mum. For herself. For everything lost and forgotten. For everything that she had taken for granted before they slipped away from her.

For the truth she had been seeking everywhere even though it had been right in front of her this entire time, only a few paces ahead. And she had chased it through bubbles and clouds and rabbit holes and driven it up a wall until Gaia had called her out on it.

By laying bare her own rage, Gaia had compelled Heidi to see what had truly happened to Leo. And so Heidi cried because now she could admit to herself that it wasn't Leo she had set out in search of. It was this moment of truth she had been running away from.

And even now she couldn't bring herself to see everything as it truly was. All she wanted was to hold on to any sliver of hope, no matter how fragile, how false, as long as it promised to lead her to Leo.

Oh, how she wanted to turn the clocks widdershins with all her might and go back in time. She wanted to run into the blue woods behind her home, Leo yipping and bounding ahead of her, until they reached the edge of the turquoise lake that was somehow always hidden until they arrived, as if the waters were waiting to reveal themselves to the girl and the dog, their own secret place no one else knew about. Leo, panting and drooling, always the first to jump into the waters like a ray of light bursting through the clouds. Heidi, following without a second thought.

This is what summer afternoons were meant for. To grow wings and fly. To grow scales and breathe underwater. And when spent from having fun, to crawl back ashore and lay out a picnic mat and eat ham sandwiches and drink ginger beer. And when sated, to let the restless, rustling leaves lull them to sleep. Then, to wake up when the breeze turned cool, and to run back home laughing and shrieking delightedly as squirrels tried to grab leftovers from their picnic basket and Leo pretend-chased them in and out of trees.

No watch to tell them the time but somehow they always made it back home just as the star of the day slipped behind the woods and the first star of the evening peeped through the sky, hesitantly at first, then more assuredly as its companions began to arrive, their party having only just begun.

Back home, a scrumptious meal, the most succulent bit of which was the cake or the mug of hot chocolate that inevitably followed.

Lying under the blankets by the window, her head on her mother's lap, Leo at her feet, outside a shapeshifting moon taking the stars for a night walk in the skies. Mother delicately running her fingers through Heidi's hair as if they were precious threads of silk, singing a lullaby that had no name and whose words Heidi could never remember.

Funny, Heidi thought, she didn't know it back then but there she was, already in the place that she was now seeking. A place where there was no trouble. Her happy place. Her safe place.

For a moment, Heidi's heart ached with the longing to go back to her childhood home, back into the woods. Something that didn't make sense if she thought about it too much told her she'd find Leo there.

But something else that was more believable told her she could go back right to the edge of the turquoise lake and dive straight in but nothing would be the same. Leo was gone. Mother was gone. And that Heidi of eleven years ago was gone too.

All she might find, if she were lucky enough, were the memories and echoes of a child's laughter and a dog's bark, their conversations in a language indecipherable to outsiders, keepsakes the woods would be unwilling to part with. But these too would be tainted by her visit, by the sense of loss now reinforced, by the realization that everything and everyone that really mattered have truly gone and were never coming back.

No. It didn't make sense to go backwards. To go looking for something that was irretrievably lost was a fool's errand. She had to look ahead, keep moving, past all the pain, and the loss. She couldn't keep whirling and meandering in her grief forever now, could she?

"Mumma," she finally spoke. Her throat hurt and her voice was raw and sounded like it belonged to a child who was lost and scared but was trying to be brave. "Mumma, I've made up my mind. When all this is over, I am going to set up a shelter for lost animals. Wouldn't that be a wonderful thing? I will dedicate my life to providing a home for homeless and lost and wandering creatures. I quite imagine it would end up becoming a zoo of some sort!" Heidi almost laughed.

"That sounds like precisely the kind of thing you will excel at, sweetheart," her mother encouraged her.

Heidi wiped away her tears. Her cheeks felt hot and flushed but now a newfound enthusiasm, a sense of purpose was taking root within her. It grew so strong so quickly she was almost giddy with optimism. She was fidgety now, her fingers itching to grasp a pencil and jot down plans on a piece of paper.

"Hmm ... Maybe it won't be a place for them to stay permanently. Perhaps it would be wiser to set this up as a temporary shelter until they are adopted and resettled in other loving homes. Some of the wilder ones could perhaps be released into the woods when they are ready. Oh Mumma, I am so excited simply thinking about this I'm getting goosebumps now." Heidi held out her hand as she spoke. Every cell in her body throbbed with excitement and pulsed against her skin. After days of despair and desperation, she felt as if she was on the cusp of something new, something hopeful, something joyful.

And that brought with it the strength to finally verbalize the question she couldn't even bear to contemplate the possibility of until recently.

"Is Leo with you, Mumma?" Heidi asked.

A pause.

Followed by a soft sigh.

Heidi held her breath.

"He is safe, honey," her mother replied.

Dissatisfied as she was with her mother's response, it occurred to Heidi then that this was the closest she had gotten to accepting the truth about Leo in her journey so far.

Until now, everyone she had met had been terribly good with words, at stringing words and constructing sentences that could have meant nothing or anything at all. Then again, maybe all that vagueness had helped her cope. Perhaps she hadn't been ready to hear the truth.

Now she was unlikely to get any closer to it, she realized, unless she willed herself to scratch just a little bit more beneath the surface.

Sooner or later, Heidi would have to make peace with the facts that Leo was gone, that she didn't know where he was, and that there was nothing she could do about it.

If Leo was safe, even if he wasn't with her, well wasn't that some consolation? Surely that was a good thing in the overall scheme of things, wasn't it?

She had to move on, Heidi reminded herself. Move on from dwelling on Leo. There was still so much from the past to be sorted out, loose ends to be tied up, knots to be unravelled, all the wrong deeds to be undone, all the good stuff that was only thought about and still needed to be said in words or in ways that another person could understand.

"Mumma," she called out again, suddenly remembering she had, as always, not inquired after her. She wanted to ask, "Are *you* alright?", then realized she had never, ever asked her mother that question growing up.

And in the years when mother was fading away in life and strength, people, sensible, wise, kind people would come to visit her mother and inquire, "Are you alright?"

And Heidi would look at them and wonder if they were being facetious. How could you ask someone if they were OK when everything about their appearance, their surroundings was utterly wrong, just the opposite of being all right?

Instead, she asked, "What's it like, Mumma? Do you like it up there … there … wherever you are now?"

She could almost see her mum shrug in that yes-of-course-everything's-great-and-what-made-you-think-otherwise manner.

"It's different," her mother replied simply. "But as with everything else in life and beyond, it's not too bad once you get used to it. Quite nice, actually."

Heidi knew what her mum was implying. That she could get used to living without Leo. She was now used to living without her mum, wasn't she? Even though at one time the very idea had been inconceivable.

"What do I do now, mum? Where do I go from here?"

"Go back home, Heidi. You have wandered long and far enough. You have met many people, been to several new places, seen many new things. You are a different person now than the Heidi who ran into the woods one evening in search of Leo. Go home now, my baby. Take all of these experiences and thoughts and emotions and wonders and dreams with you, and build your life anew."

"Will I not be abandoning Leo then?"

"You have done all you could, baby. But you can't go on searching forever. Mortals do not have the luxury of forever, honey. You have to stop somewhere. And only you can decide where."

"But what if I am wrong, mumma?"

"My sweet, sweet child, you will never know if you were right or wrong, and you will have to live with that, the not knowing. Wondering if you should have turned left instead of right. Wishing you had turned just one more corner. And who knows, maybe you would have found Leo there. Or maybe not. But there is no way to tell, darling. That is the anguish we all have to live with. You may not agree with me now, but that is what makes life beautiful. This element of doubt. The lingering uncertainty. In the mystery lies the answer, my beautiful, beautiful child. Don't you see? Each joy is sweeter for all the sorrows that preceded it. Each quest is made more delightful by everything that was sacrificed along the way."

Heidi sighed. "I think I understand what you are saying. But my heart aches terribly all the same, Mumma. I don't think I can ever love anyone again as much as I loved Leo."

"No one will replace Leo, my darling. No one has to. But you will find new and different ways to love, Heidi. Your heart will grow tender with every ache that presses upon it."

As fantastic as her mother's words sounded to her, Heidi believed them. She clung on to this newfound hope with the desperation of a fish that had been washed ashore and was now imploring the waves to drag it back out to the sea. In the company of her mother, Heidi felt strong and brave. She did not want the conversation to end. The telephone booth had become a portal, transporting her to a world that promised her joy after sorrow, solace after grief, peace after loss. She feared that the instant she hung up, the words and their import would disappear like thieves slinking away from the moonlight into the shadows. And even if she were to somehow remember and repeat her mother's messages verbatim, they would sound hollow and foolish to her own ears.

"I will do as you say, Mumma," she finally said. "I will go back home. But not tonight, Mumma. I am very tired. Will you please stay with me until I fall asleep?"

And she allowed herself to slide down to the floor, tucked her legs under her, and leaned against the wall, cradling the phone between her ear and shoulder. She closed her eyes and her mother hummed her favourite lullaby.

And Heidi thought about the blue woods and the emerald lake and Leo and stars in the summertime. And for the first time since Leo went missing, she drifted off into a brief but dreamless sleep.

CHAPTER 9
WINGS AND ROOTS, A NEW HEART, AND THE GYPSY

The river flowed placidly, breaking up the reflection of the new moon into smithereens of blue silver. A small boat moored to the near bank bobbed gently.

An old woman leaned over the edge of the boat, cradling half an oyster shell in her hand. She dipped the shell in the water. A tiny orb of moon-silver floated into it. The old woman produced another half shell and cupped the first. She pressed her lips to the edges of the two half shells, and they clasped shut, like a jewel box aglow with pearly moonlight from within. She let it slip from her hands into the water, like a prayer, an offering, and watched it sink to the bottom of the river.

"There. Now they are in a place where the darkness gobbles up all the light," the gypsy said triumphantly.

"Or maybe there, far beyond the reaches of our vision, the light grows stronger, one orb after another, and dispels the darkness. And we will learn of it much, much later," Heidi wondered aloud.

The gypsy sighed. "Sometimes the world suffers from too

much light. We can all do with some darkness now and then. Our eyes get accustomed to the dark, but never to too much light."

She turned around and beckoned Heidi over. Heidi climbed into the boat and sat across from the gypsy, their knees touching, each able to hear the sound of the soft breaths and heartbeats of the other louder than their own.

"You are not one of those pretentious torch-bearers, are you?" the gypsy asked, but without waiting for an answer, leaned forward and peered at Heidi as if she was making up her mind about something.

Her feline eyes grew greener and greener as she searched Heidi's face, then grabbed her palms and read between the lines. Eventually satisfied, she drew back and said, "No. You are no torch-bearer. You are a lover of the dark. You have jumped into its depths and have allowed your heart and soul to be imbued with the black bane. And you have found it can be good just as it can be bad. And that is why your heart glows, with light made brighter by the darkness surrounding it. Not unlike my moon orbs in the oyster shells," she chuckled and gestured grandly towards the waters.

"I do feel different," Heidi admitted. "I know I am not the same I was before … before I set out in search of Leo. But now I am going back home, back to where all this started but as a different person, and part of me does not want to go back there. Part of me, perhaps it is the dark, shadowy part that you speak of, wants to keep meandering. Just so I won't have to go back home and see that he has really gone."

"So you want to lead a gypsy's life?" the old woman cackled.

Heidi smiled. "Is that why you don't settle down someplace permanently?"

The gypsy wagged a bony finger at her. "The only thing that settles down is dust, love," she said. "The world is forever changing. So are we. So are You. So am I. We are never the same one moment to the next. So what is this permanence that you talk about when life itself is so fleeting?"

"But isn't it scary to not have a place to call home? To not have a place to go back to?"

The gypsy waved a hand dismissively. "Your home has changed too, my love. It is a different home now with Leo not there. It is a different place now that you have changed. But you already knew this. You didn't need me to tell you all this."

Heidi nodded. "These thoughts, these are foremost on my mind now. But these are new thoughts to me. I find myself in strange, unfamiliar territory. I had never considered life without Leo. Never had reason to. In some ways, this has been much more difficult than the time I lost my mother."

A sense of restless urgency swept up her spine. As if there was somewhere else she needed to be this very instant. As if a thousand little birds, winged pixies of bronze and brass and copper and gold, were fluttering inside of her, looking for a way out. They wanted to take her with them, let her ride on their backs, and they would all soar across the mountains and the seas, and who could stop them from tumbling into other galaxies and universes, and perhaps they would be the first to find out the names of UFOs and determine what aliens from other worlds thought about this little blue and green orb they all had once lived in.

"On the one hand," Heidi continued, "I think I ought to be responsible, go back home, and turn this life-altering incident into something meaningful, something purposeful. Why, just the other day I was thinking of setting up a shelter for lost animals. When this idea first popped into my mind, I couldn't wait to get started. But my enthusiasm grows and wanes as it pleases. One instant I feel I can't wait to get started on this idea. And the very next instant I wish to have nothing to do with this project. Leo's gone and I don't want to spend a lifetime reliving that loss through others' experiences. On the other hand, there is this little selfish desire growing inside me. You see, all these years I have been homebound because of Leo. The farthest I have ventured from my cottage is to the neighbouring village where my a friend lives. Now I see no further reason for me to stay at home. I'd like to travel some more, meet some interesting people, tumble into adventures, have some fun ..."

"And kiss handsome strangers while you are at it," the gypsy interjected with a smile.

Heidi blushed. But the more she thought about it, the more certain she grew that she wanted to neither keep looking for Leo nor go back to her cottage in the village. She detested herself for using the word but Leo's departure had provided her with an 'opportunity', a chance as it were to try something new, something different.

"As you must," the gypsy continued. "Heidi, no matter what you have seen or heard until now, take it from this old woman as the truth, you cannot have wings and roots at the same time. Nature will ensure you evolve in such a way that you enhance what you use the most and give up what you have no use for. Otherwise you will become extinct. Like dragons and dinosaurs. Look at the birds soaring high in the skies, settling into their nests when dusk falls over the world.

But they too know that when the time comes, they must migrate. It is a question of survival. Look at the trees, rooted to the same spot for an entire lifetime. The ones that endure have learnt how to shed their leaves and raise their naked branches to pay tribute to the endless winter. You have to choose, Heidi. What do you want? Wings? Or roots? Would you rather make that choice of your own volition or have it forced upon you by circumstance or chance?"

A light breeze picked up and rippled the waters. The boat started to float downstream. They glided past the dark, still shapes of the night adorning the riverbanks and beyond.

"Our true homes reside here, Heidi," the gypsy patted her own chest. "We carry our homes with us wherever we go. We wander not because we are lost, but because the world is vast and life is short, so it does not matter whether the paths we set out on are straight or curved or meandering or crooked or loop back into themselves and cannot be neatly plotted on a map. In a way, we all are still frogs in a well. It's just that some of us believe we have much larger wells than others do."

She shuffled closer to Heidi and said, "Please allow me ..." And before Heidi could ask or say anything in response, the old woman pressed her fingers against Heidi's chest. Heidi looked down in time to see a little orb of moonlight slip through her blouse and skin, and unexpectedly warm the cockles of her heart.

"There. We could all do with new beginnings from time to time," the gypsy smiled.

CHAPTER 10

SOLSTICE, THE MARKET SQUARE, AND THE TRUTH

The world appeared a little different to Heidi when she woke up the next morning. Her bedroom was suffused with warm sunlight, as it was every morning. But only today did she pause to notice how the sunbeams glinted off surfaces of wood and metal and glass and made her room sparkle like a gemstone. Downstairs, looking out the kitchen windows into her backyard and the woods beyond, she saw how daylight and leaf-shadow danced to a melodic mélange of birdsongs.

She opened the front door and saw Leo's leash lying on the porch. A squiggly sash of brown on white floorboards. Abandoned. It looked like a dead snake. It was still hooked to the collar at one end. Missing its wearer, the contraption looked like a lasso, Heidi noticed not for the first time. It was limp and useless now, with no one to rein in. As if the old boy had somehow shrunk and wriggled out of the restraint and had bounded away towards mischief.

The thought made her smile. Yes, that certainly sounded like the kind of no-good that Leo would get up to.

Heidi picked up the leash and wound it around her wrist. It was best to return it to Leo, she decided.

It was early evening by the time Heidi set out. The solstitial sun had been shining generously on the market square for several hours now. It was his longest day out, and nearly the entire village had gathered to make merry at the square and bask in his warmth. An afternoon of festivity and enjoyment was now segueing into an evening of more dancing and drinking with so much gusto that Heidi, stepping into the square, wondered if the party had only just begun.

Temporary stalls had cropped up under strings of colourful pennants and offered whimsical wares and splendid services. A child sat still as a stone in one. An artist hunched over and dusted the child's face with the intense, brilliant hues of a butterfly's wings. One last stroke with a flourish and the artist stood back and folded her arms. The child stood up, flapped her arms and poof! A butterfly flitted out of a dust of colours and skittered above and beyond the pennants and treetops and clouds.

"Mesdames, Messieurs, poppets and imps, mischief-makers and trouble-seekers," a man hollered out from a neighbouring stall. "Come and choose a dream or two, one drop from the past, a few swigs of the future." Iridescent fluids swirled within bottles and jars and vials and tubes of myriad dimensions that hovered in the stall as if neatly stacked on invisible shelves. Small and large boxes rattled in a corner like jiggling maracas.

"Which dream will you choose today, my little poppet?" the man gesticulated grandly. There was something very familiar about him but was it his voice, or the way he tilted his head, or how he lifted a single eyebrow eloquently that roused a feeling of déja vu in Heidi, she couldn't say precisely.

A number of bottles and jars floated past, bearing curious labels that reminded Heidi of the bedtime stories her mother concocted on the nights the child demanded a new tale, something unheard of, something unfamiliar, a story that would play tricks with her mind and plant strange and exotic dreams in it for the night. *A well-worn whimsy. A piece of sky. Discount dreams. The hidden moon. Half a sun. Dreams of a newborn.*

Heidi was quite tempted to pick a dream, to let some unknown wonder choose her, and follow it to the end of the world. But there were more pressing matters to attend to. She will come back here another time, she promised herself.

She went around the maple tree that stood in the centre of the market square. Its leaves were the colour of earth and fire and sunset. As if the Universe wanted to strike up a conversation with her, the tree dropped a leaf on to Heidi's shoulder as she passed under it. As Heidi picked the leaf, it crumbled into golden fall-dust in her palm. Where she sprinkled it on the ground sprung up plumes of flame-coloured celosia flowers. They formed a path that led her to the florist's.

Heidi chose an assortment of golden-yellow flowers. A tall, slender girl with beads threaded through her long, thick plaits, deftly and delicately arranged peonies, calla lilies, freesias, daffodils, buttercups, primroses and snapdragons around a single strelitzia. A bird of paradise perched atop an explosion of fiery golden blooms.

To a casual observer, it would have appeared as if the bird was about to fly away in a trail of pollen and gold dust towards paradise. To Heidi, it meant that this, right here was where paradise was, in the midst of a golden bouquet of flowers. In her small hands, cupped together, as if she was about to make an offering of her grief, as if she was about to receive a gift, a new lease on life. Paradise was in her little heart.

It was only now that she saw how large the teeny thing really was, her little heart, how much grief and pain and hope and love could fit into its throbbing form and yet leave enough room for new love to enter and settle down beside all the old and buried ones.

The florist was saying something that Heidi didn't hear, so she didn't move when the girl cut a strand of raven hair from her head, beads intact, and placed it on Heidi's palm. The tress wound around Heidi's wrist and clasped itself. The beads pressed into Heidi's skin and disappeared into her flesh, leaving behind an indelible pattern of black ink, a string of alphabets in cursive hand that said only one word. 'Leo'. The curlicues of 'L' and 'o' looped around her wrist, and now everything that was essential was contained within that one word inked on hand.

"It's beautiful," Heidi gasped. "But now you've made it impossible to forget. How will I let go now?"

The girl laid her hand on Heidi's. "To let go of does not mean to forget. In fact, it is only when you've made the most wonderful memories with each other that you can bid farewell without regret."

Heidi had to agree. She and Leo couldn't have been happier even if they had tried.

~

Leo was buried atop a small hill that rose gently from the edge of the village. His grave was a small mound of brown earth dug not too long ago.

Heidi's fingers tingled at the memory of scooping out smatterings of earth with her bare hands as Leo had lain cold and unmoving next to her. The white pebbles she had pressed gently into the ground, spelling out his name at the foot of his grave, were undisturbed.

Crowning his resting place was a large, evergreen oak tree. From its branches hung wind chimes that caught the light of the sun and the voice of the wind and transformed them into soft tinkles that cavorted like butterflies and bubbles and lullabies in the air.

"Hey, you," Heidi whispered at first, so as to not disturb Leo in his slumber. But she was pretty sure he must have cocked a ear at the sound of her voice, an unexpected cross-beat dropped into the euphony of tinkles, so she continued, "I've brought you the second most beautiful thing in the world." Her voice caught in her throat.

Before they could fall from her clumsy grip, she placed the bunch of golden yellow flowers on the mound of earth. The air was so thick with the delicious fragrance of the blooms she knew that Leo would be able to taste their scent on his tongue.

She stepped up to the tree and deposited Leo's leash and collar into a hollow not far above his resting place. Her hands suddenly felt empty as if she had nothing more to give, for everything had already been taken away from her.

The tears she had expected didn't appear. A long time ago she had read in a book, the name of which she couldn't recall now, that tears run away with the memories of the loved one.

And sure enough, for all the tears she had shed since the last time she was here, Heidi had filled her head with thoughts and dreams and questions and befuddlements and analyses and explanations, everything to do with Leo but very little about Leo himself. The irony made her laugh out loud.

She worked back through the clutter in her mind and recalled the last time she had pressed her face against Leo's unconscious back, his belly heaving softly beneath her cheek, the drug creeping through his veins to his heart, the silence between breaths gently surging and billowing until the quietness was all that remained.

Other memories now came flooding into her head. Happy memories. Of summer afternoons in the woods. Of ice creams and squirrels. Of a jack-o'-lantern bobbing about on four paws. Of cookie jar muzzles. Memories that smelt of freshly mowed grass and tasted like dewdrops. Memories of all the happiness two mortal souls could possibly share with each other in a lifetime. Because, to each, the other had been the most beautiful being in the world.

The man had been waiting for her at a deferential distance. Heidi didn't notice him until she had turned away from Leo's grave and had started to walk downhill. He emerged from a clump of trees, and Heidi realized she had been peering into the thicket almost expecting to find him there.

He was intensely familiar yet utterly forgettable. Ordinary looking but Heidi couldn't tell how old he was. He was dressed in a nondescript white tee and black jacket over blue jeans, an attire she wouldn't have noticed had she not been looking.

She knew this man. They had met before, she was certain. She snatched at the memory but the harder she tried to recollect, the more rapidly it slipped away from her grasp. Like a dream disappearing beyond the edge of consciousness.

Of course! Dreams! It was the man who had been selling dreams at the stall in the market square. The man who had accidentally run over Gaia's Leo. The man who had been the first to tell her to let go.

A feeling of déja vu rushed over Heidi and another distant memory surfaced. Nine afternoons ago, after she had buried Leo and had started to walk downhill, a man, the same person standing in front of her now, had emerged from this very clump of trees.

Her mind had been so full of thoughts of Leo's death that she had only half-heard what the man had had to say. But, she remembered, he had been very kind to her then as he was now.

The Dream Pedlar, were the only words he had said by way of introduction. He had then pressed into her hand a heart-shaped bottle of frosted glass. In it had swished a liquid of Prussian blue. A silver crescent had surfaced from within and revealed itself occasionally, a tiny glint of argent light that disappeared almost as soon as it glittered.

"The Hidden Moon," he had prescribed.

A remedy for pain and sorrow. A febrifuge for grief.

A potion that Heidi had swilled down without much thought.

And then the dreams had begun.

CHAPTER 11

EXPLANATIONS, ENLIGHTENMENTS, AND YET ANOTHER QUEST

The Dream Pedlar was handsome in a roguish way. Heidi looked at him askance as they strolled downhill back towards the village square.

She wondered why she had never noticed that before. It also occurred to her she might not even remember this observation after they parted from this encounter.

It was strange then how she could remember all the dreams with alarming alacrity. As if they had been real. Real enough to touch and taste, to hide under her skin and wiggle in her brain.

"Your belief in something is what makes it real," the Dream Pedlar explained.

"So are you saying these were not merely dreams? That the Oldest Witch, the huntsman, Gaia, Mr. Fox … and all the others … they all exist somewhere in the woods?" Heidi asked.

"Yes, and no," the Dream Pedlar replied. "If you go looking for them, believing they exist, you will find them. Oh, you will find them alright. Because they will come looking for you.

They like the seekers, the believers, the dreamers. For who cares about the truth if not the seeker? How can a dream exist without a dreamer? What is a myth without a believer? It is our belief in them that keeps them from becoming extinct. But if you set forth with a cynical mind, you will not be able to see them even if they came right up to you and shook their fists under your nose."

As Heidi tried to understand, more questions and ideas popped into her mind. She was a student now, eager to learn, driven to ponder over and understand, anxious to unravel the meaning of her recent encounters. "Looking back now, I think in some ways they mirrored me, my feelings and emotions. For a long time, I couldn't accept that Leo was dead even though I had buried him with my own hands. I was in denial. And that is when I met the Oldest Witch. She too was living in a bubble of her own. And the Omniscient Man. It was because I couldn't truly accept the enormity of my loss." She looked at the Dream Pedlar for confirmation, validation of her hypothesis.

"That is so," he replied. "Everyone you met, and their stories, all reflected your own journey on the path of grief."

More understanding dawned on Heidi. "And they all knew Leo had died, which is why not one of them gave me any hints as to his whereabouts. Of course, I too had always known, hadn't I? Only I kept denying it, telling myself that I'd find him if only I looked hard enough."

And the Dream Pedlar talked. And Heidi listened. About the dreams he had shown her. And what they had meant.

Fuhen, the beautiful Siberian Husky, on a leash. Leo's leash. Oh, how Heidi's state of denial had instilled in her the conviction that she would find Leo and bring him back home. Fuhen lunging at her ankle. Heidi's world had been rattled by Leo's disappearance, and her feelings were about to become unmoored.

She had then tried to shush her heart for a brief while, erase her grief by turning her attention to the overwhelming pains of the world around her, as the Omniscient Man had shown her.

But her had sorrow stood its ground and refused to go away, like a lighthouse on the shore, drawing all attention to itself. How could another's pain invalidate her sense of loss?

And she had no choice but to succumb to all the inexplicable feelings that had invaded her. As she had, in the presence of the huntsman.

Like a pendulum she had swung from laughter, that extreme of all emotions, to a brief semblance of equanimity, only to fall down the rabbit hole. Up the emotional seesaw she had veered again, kissing a stranger and setting free that tiny part of herself that acknowledged the truth about Leo and had wanted to move on.

Then the anger. The rage that she had held on to like a crutch as she stumbled and hobbled towards a new phase of life.

"Anger is good," the Dream Pedlar said. "It comes when you stop wondering how you could possibly carry on without the one you lost. It helps you survive. But like most forms of power, it can quickly become abusive."

"Which is why you insisted I let go," Heidi said. "Let go of that rage, that bitterness before it blew out of proportion and incinerated everything that came in its way." Gaia. And how she had forced Heidi to confront the truth of Leo's demise. But her rage was all that Heidi had chosen to notice and judge.

Mumma on the telephone. Heidi's newfound enthusiasm for life. She laughed now at her naïve plans to set up an animal shelter. The mere thought of such an ambitious undertaking sapped her energy now. But then the gypsy had given her a new heart, one that was better able to tide over the constant vicissitude of emotions without crumbling into pieces.

One more fragment of a sentence came to memory now from a faraway place and time.

Life, worth fighting for, the Dream Pedlar had said at their very first encounter. But it wasn't Leo's life he had been talking about. It was hers.

Heidi had been standing atop a precarious precipice, one foot on the ground, one in the air, having made up her mind to follow Leo to the grave. And her faithful dog had come along to save her in his own way. Not from her grief. No. That was her own to dive and sink into, to explore and be overwhelmed by, and to finally prevail over. There was no other way. The metamorphosis was hers alone to experience. But it was in searching for Leo that she had found herself. In not finding him again, she had been saved.

Heidi couldn't help but marvel at the beauty of it all as it unfolded in front of her. Like a parchment of sheet music that demystified the romance of sound and silence, untangling the intertwined, laying bare the secrets of their liaison, but only just. So much of the magic still lay in the hands that bowed the strings, how could there be only one rendition, only one interpretation, a single version of the truth?

And so she asked questions and sought answers, and was enlightened at every turn in ways she didn't anticipate. Each explanation was like a surprise gift, the unraveling offering as much joy as the treasure hidden within.

Her heart sank when the pennants fluttering above the market square finally came into view. The conversation, the delight of discovery was nearing its end. There was still one tiny aspect that Heidi wanted to seek clarification on.

"Mr. Fox," she said. "He is a silver fox, isn't he?"

The Dream Pedlar shook his head. "Oh no no. He is a red fox. The largest of the true foxes," he said, and looked at her expectantly.

Heidi felt a sense of urgency shoot up her spine. "I must be off then," she said. "I have work to do."

"I was hoping you'd embark on that journey," the Dream Pedlar said, looking pleased with himself but only for a moment. His face fell the very next instant. "Mr. Fox will be glad to see you again. Very glad, I have no doubt about that. But many dangers lurk on this path. Terrors and perils await you on this journey," he cautioned.

"I have nothing more to lose," Heidi shrugged.

The Dream Pedlar smiled a sad but comprehending smile. "He still wonders, and so do I, whether you either possess extraordinary courage or are an utter imbecile. Remember, I am only a dream away."

~

Back home, Heidi found her knapsack behind the door. Neatly packed in it was a torch, a loaf of bread left over from yesterday's supper, two bars of Mars chocolate, a flask of spiced tea, and a bottle of water. She remembered to throw in spare batteries for the torch.

She heaved her bag on to her shoulder and made for the back door. The last time she had undertaken this journey, Leo had been foremost on her mind. This time she was thinking about a different canid. Mr. Fox.

Beautiful, isn't it? Those had been his first words to her. What had he been commenting on, Heidi now wondered. The silver mask of moonlight that had shrouded everything in the woods, including him? Or the beginning of her journey?

Leo. That had been her first word to him, and she wondered if that had been an indication of things to come, a clue to the present journey she was setting out on.

She recalled his words now. *The right place is the one where you will stop looking for him. Until you get there, every place will feel wrong. Very wrong.*

And so she had kept going on and on and on in search of Leo because she had believed that when she reached the right place, she would find him there.

She had ploughed on through every dimension of space and time and emotion and being, no matter how wrong they had seemed. But the right place had been here all along, right in the home she had once shared with Leo, the place she had come back to when she decided to stop looking for him, the place where she finally accepted his loss and agreed to let go.

And then a thought struck her. Maybe it wasn't so much about the place at all as it had been about her. She was a different person now than the Heidi who had run away from Leo's death on the evening of his burial. A different version of her own self. The same old Heidi but who now tilted her head at a different angle so she could see things from a hidden point of view, who now befriended vagueness and uncertainty so that she could pull them along with her on her path and not let them hold her back.

In learning to let go, she realized she was the one moving on, not the one left behind. She wasn't the child clinging to a torn kite that would no longer fly when he tugged. She was the kite itself. She was the one with the wings. And now, even with broken wings, she would fly again wherever she pleased, her orbit no longer defined by the length of the reel or the skill of the kite flyer. No place could ever be wrong for the free soul. It was its own right place, its own home, wherever it went.

And in her willingness to embrace what lay in front of her eyes, Heidi had been endowed with the rare gift of clear sight. All the sounds and colours of the world were now coming alive for her as she began to behold all the magic and beauty manifesting around her. She could now see birdsongs floating on the breeze and hear the colours of the rainbow exploding in the skies.

And this new, but old, Heidi saw with new eyes what she had previously missed. The mischief of the moonlight that had turned the red fox into a silver fox. The red fox the huntsman was scouring the woods for.

Mr. Fox likely knew the huntsman was on his tail. The trees would have spread the word. But Heidi didn't want to take any chances. She had already lost Leo. Here was an opportunity to save the life of another, and she wasn't about to squander it now and repent later.

She looked around the house one last time. The last of the

sunlight streamed in through the windows and clung to dust motes that spiralled upwards. They looked like tiny fireflies of the daytime. Everything else lay pale and still. Forgotten. Like an absence. Leo's. And soon, her's. With the sight of the gleaming, dancing specks of dust firmly imprinted in her mind, Heidi let herself out through the back door.

Some things hadn't changed. It was still impossible to tell where her backyard ended and where the woods began. The evening sky was beautiful as always in that transient, hesitant way that makes something eternally exquisite.

It brought something to Heidi's memory and she rummaged in her knapsack. Tucked away into one of the inner pockets was a heart-shaped bottle of frosted glass wrapped inside a piece of black fabric. The hidden moon in a piece of night sky. One, a gift from the Dream Pedlar. The other, a gift from the Oldest Witch.

Heidi tossed the cloth towards her cottage. It caught in the wind and flew up to the roof. Stars swooped down from the twilight skies above, like birds hurrying to their evening roosts, and garlanded the eaves the way Heidi used to hang fairy lights on occasion.

She opened the bottle, now nearly empty. And a crescent moon glided out towards the rooftop and came to rest on the chimney, settling there as if she never intended to leave. And Heidi realized she would never have any trouble finding her way back home.

It was funny how her life had come full circle, Heidi thought, as she made for the woods. Today was not entirely unlike the day she saw Leo's leash and collar lying abandoned on the porch and had run wildly into the woods.

There was a small difference though. The last time she had been running away. This time she knew where she was headed.

And she pushed ahead courageously, one step after another, one foot in wakefulness, the other in a dream.

ENJOYED IN SEARCH OF LEO?

Thank you for reading In Search of Leo!

If you loved the book, I hope you will consider writing a short review—even a simple line or two—on the site where you bought the book.

Publishing is still driven by word of mouth, and when you leave a review it helps other readers decide this is a book worth reading. Thank you for your help in spreading the word.

You can also sign up to my monthly newsletter to read a bonus chapter, titled *'The Dance of the Mad Man'*.

https://thedreampedlar.com/fiction-the-dance-of-the-mad-man/

When you sign up, you will also receive access to additional works of fiction available exclusively to subscribers.

AUTHOR'S NOTE

Dear Reader,

Thank you for finding me here at last, after the end of a story I hope you loved reading.

In Search of Leo is my debut work of fiction, and it first went out into the world exactly five years ago.

I have written several books and stories since then, and knowing what I know now, I don't think I'd dare to write something like *In Search of Leo* ever again.

As a writer who knows a teensy bit more (yet far too little) about storytelling now than I did back then, I'd be too worried about sticking to the technicalities and conventions of storytelling to write something as experiential and meandering and experimental as I hope this tale was.

Yet, I take immense pride in this first book that not only marked my foray into self-publishing but also helped me cope with my own grief during a very distressing period.

I first got the idea for the story in February 2016 when I was only four months pregnant and had been sentenced to bedrest for the remainder of my pregnancy owing to a very high risk of premature delivery.

It was a difficult time to say the least, made even more difficult by all the advice and suggestions I received from well-meaning family members and friends on coping in this stressful situation.

The suggestions ranged from praying to God to bribing him with a promise of some future offering, from distraction to denial, and from expressions of helplessness to hopefulness.

I conjured up some of the characters — the Oldest Witch, the Omniscient Man, Gaia, to name a few — based on these conversations.

My initial plan was to write a book on how not to console someone in a time of difficulty because none of the advice I was receiving resonated with me.

Also, I hadn't yet learnt how to touch my own pain and be with it, without wishing or demanding that I were someone else in some place else doing something else and not stuck in that hospital bed in Sydney for weeks and weeks, waking up each morning and hoping that wouldn't be the day little D would choose to be born prematurely and worrying about how I'd cope if such an eventuality came to pass.

It didn't. D was born close to his due date and in good health, and he remains one of the most delightful, wonderful and sacred blessings of my life to this day.

My true, swift and slippery descent into grief began a few months after he was born.

Postpartum depression and anxiety. Moving back from Australia to Canada. Abhinav and I looking after the little infant all by ourselves without family or friends to lean on.

Choosing to be a stay-at-home mother and grieving the alternate, un-lived lives I was leaving behind, especially as friends and family questioned my choice often, and I found myself more riddled with doubt and anxiety and robbed of faith and conviction than I had ever been in all my life.

It was during the first eighteen months of D's life that I wrote this story. By then, it was no longer a sermon on how not to talk to someone going through a difficult time. It had become an exploration of all the feelings I was feeling back then.

Feelings I didn't know how to label. Feelings I had no names for. Feelings that came unannounced, without reason, without mercy. Feelings that I felt 'wrong' about feeling, because I shouldn't have been feeling that way, isn't it?

Feelings that I didn't talk to anybody about because I didn't want any of the usual but unhelpful 'pray to God' or 'it's just a phase' or 'everybody goes through this' responses.

Feelings that I eventually coped with by writing about them with the help of the characters in this story.

Looking back now, I am amazed that the story I wrote in the midst of some very dark times to make sense of all the pain and despair turned out to be one of acceptance and hope.

One observation that my wise editor, Sarah Chorn, kept making as she edited my initial draft was that it wasn't very clear to her whether Heidi's encounters with the eccentric characters in the woods were dreams or not, nor could she tell exactly when Heidi slipped into and out of these dreams if that's they were.

She had suggested that I clarify those entry and exit points to the reader to explain that these encounters were dream-states, if that's how I intended to portray them.

I thought about her wise suggestion a lot, but in the end I decided to not make the beginnings and endings of each chapter any less vague.

I wasn't writing a portal fantasy. This tale is an exploration of grief, and as I mentioned in the foreword, grief is a meandering that happens of its own accord, seemingly without purpose or reason.

Any of its constituent feelings comes without announcement and doesn't bid you farewell when it departs.

And that was the time when I began to learn that we rarely see anyone or anything as it is.

Everything we perceive is through our own unique lenses of biases and prejudices, our past experiences and conditioning, our beliefs and hopes, all of which make up who we are and how we see ourselves and the world around us.

In that sense, everything is an illusion. Everything is *maya*.

Which begets the questions: What is reality? And what is a dream? Where does one end and the other begin?

I was so thrilled at finally having had a sliver of understanding of this concept that I wanted to share that with whoever happened to read this book.

And so I chose to not clarify which parts of Heidi's experiences were real and which were dreams. That is something I've left for each of you to decide for yourself.

If that compromised the pleasure of reading this book for you, I apologize and assure you that wasn't my intention at all.

And if this book resonated with you and helped you make sense of and accept your own sorrows a little more than before, than I've been amply rewarded for my efforts. Thank you.

We've come together so far, and I hope you would like to stay connected with me.

I send out a monthly newsletter on the last Sunday of every month. Subscription is free. When you sign up, you will gain exclusive access to a bonus chapter from *In Search of Leo* as well as a bunch of other short fiction available only to subscribers.

You will be the first to hear of my forthcoming works. I also include updates on my writing life, book recommendations, and occasional surprises.

Thank you for staying with me this far. If you choose to accompany me further on this journey, I promise you a magical ride.

Delightful dreams and wondrous whimsies. Impossible illusions and fleeting fantasies.

Straight from The Dream Pedlar's emporium into your mailbox!

Climb aboard at https://thedreampedlar.com/newsletter!

~ Anitha Krishnan
Burlington, Ontario
18 January 2023

ACKNOWLEDGEMENTS

My dear friends, Karim Albatish and Lavanya Ravi, you two were the first to see the story in its initial form. Thank you for being my *beta readers* long before I even knew such a term existed. Without your inputs and encouragement, I would have simply tucked the manuscript away in a drawer and forgotten all about it. *shudder* Thank you for cheering me on!

Sarah, thank you for your wise edits and constant encouragement. You gave me invaluable support on the last leg of this story's journey to publication. Thank you!

Pen, the first time I saw the cover you had designed for the book, I was blown away. You beautifully captured both the quest-like nature of Heidi's journey as well as the poignancy of grief in that spellbinding image. Thank you! I'm just so lucky Sarah introduced me to you.

Darling Dhruv, you are the reason I wrote this book. You are the reason I finally mustered the courage to follow my heart. Thank you for coming into my life and for changing my world and my life into something so spectacular!

Dearest Abhinav, I come to you at the end but you've been with me right from the beginning of my author journey. You are a true *jeevansaathi*. Without you, I'd be meandering in countless griefs of my own making. Thank you for always choosing to see only the best in me, especially when I keep insisting on looking at only the worst. I love you with all my heart and soul.

~ Anitha Krishnan
Burlington, Ontario
18 January 2023

MORE BOOKS BY ANITHA KRISHNAN

https://thedreampedlar.com/books/

Dying Wishes

A contemporary fantasy novel weaving Hindu mythology and South Indian folklore into a quest for belonging across different worlds — the World of Mortals and the World of Gods, India and Canada, the past and the present, the world outside and the one within.

A Benevolent Goddess

A story of a goddess who is punished for her desire to help human beings but is unable to find salvation by any other means.

Erased from Existence

A paranormal mystery in which a fifteen-year-old is erased from the memories and perception of everyone. Trapped in oblivion, she quickly finds that to get out she will have to unearth and reveal long-buried family secrets. Secrets that have remained hidden for centuries.

Hello, Dreamer! Poems & Dreams

An eclectic collection of 100 short poems encompassing musings on the universe and its mysteries, nature and human life, my secret longings and fears, love and heartbreak, the sun and the moon, the stars and the seas, light and shadow, and joy and nostalgia.

ABOUT ANITHA KRISHNAN

Anitha Krishnan is a speculative fiction author and an award-winning poet. She has lived in and left pieces of her heart in many places across the world including Singapore, Australia, Canada, and most of all in her beloved birthplace, India. She presently lives in Burlington, Ontario with her husband and their cherished child.

Find more books and her blog on the writing life at
https://thedreampedlar.com.

Sign up to her monthly newsletter at
https://thedreampedlar.com/newsletter
to receive heartfelt musings, exclusive updates, book recommendations, free fiction, and more!

You can also support her work by signing up to Tales for Dreamers, a paid subscription service to receive a short original tale of wonder and whimsy every week.
https://thedreampedlar.com/tales-for-dreamers/

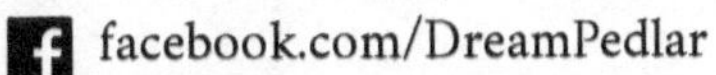 facebook.com/DreamPedlar

www.ingramcontent.com/pod-product-compliance
Lightning Source LLC
Chambersburg PA
CBHW031005210726
48290CB00007B/2485